The 1-800 -MURDERS

BY
ROBERT L. BAILEY

the Peppertree Press
Sarasota, Florida

This is a work of fiction. Names, characters, businesses, organizations, places, events and incidents either are the product of the author's imagination or used fictitiously. Any resemblance to actual persons, living or dead, events, or locales is entirely coincidental.

Copyright © Robert L. Bailey, 2013

All rights reserved. Published by the Peppertree Press, LLC.
the Peppertree Press and associated logos are trademarks of
the Peppertree Press, LLC.

No part of this publication may be reproduced, stored in a retrieval system, transmitted in any form or by any means, electronic, mechanical, photocopying, recording, or otherwise, without prior written permission of the publisher and author/illustrator.
Graphic design by Rebecca Barbier.

For information regarding permission,
call 941-922-2662 or contact us at our website:
www.peppertreepublishing.com or write to:
the Peppertree Press, LLC.
Attention: Publisher
1269 First Street, Suite 7
Sarasota, Florida 34236

ISBN: 978-1-61493-187-4

Library of Congress Number: 2013941454

Printed in the U.S.A.

Printed June 2013

ACKNOWLEDGMENTS

Special thanks go to **Lane Gutstein**, my editor. Lane has edited six of my seven books. She has improved them in so many ways, even though I make her job nearly impossible by continuing to fiddle with the manuscript until press time. The errors that remain are my own.

To **Sylvia,** my best friend and wife of 57 years, who encouraged me to try my hand at novels and who provided feedback as the story took shape.

To my daughter, **Nancy Baker**, who was the first to read the not-quite-completed manuscript. She said, "Dad, it's OK, but you can do better," which resulted in a complete re-write. Nancy, you'll like this version better.

To **Julie Ann Howell** and **Teri Franco** of Peppertree Press, who have made the publishing experience relatively painless.

You have to have sort of a twisted mind to create the kind of stuff included in my novels. To my **friends and business associates** who have said, "All along I knew you had a twisted mind." I wish you had told me earlier. I have learned so much from all of you, and I appreciate your friendship. Thank you.

Bob Bailey

1.

A blue Honda Accord stopped in front of a well-maintained two-story frame home in an upscale Pittsburgh neighborhood.

A man, probably in his late 40s or early 50s, got out of the car and walked slowly but confidently toward the front door. His demeanor was that of a professional man; he wore a dark gray suit, white shirt, red tie, and well-polished black shoes.

When he reached the front door, he stopped momentarily, removed a cloth from a small plastic bag and wiped his hands and the soles of his shoes.

He rang the bell. A man answered—early 70s, gray hair, a slight paunch from too little physical activity after retirement, but still physically and mentally active and alert.

"Mr. Edgar Wheeler?"

"Yes, I'm Ed Wheeler."

"I'm Carl Bristol. I'm the one who called you about the *Tomorrow* radio program. Thank you for agreeing to see me. May I come in?"

"Sure, come on in.

"Please sit down," Wheeler said, pointing to a beige fabric armchair in the living room. The room was well-decorated and showed it once had the benefit of a woman's touch, although the furniture was probably 20 years old. There was no obvious wear and tear. Like most living rooms, it had not been used except for special company.

"Mr. Wheeler, I am told you are a regular listener of the *Tomorrow* radio program with Mike Moseley. Is that correct?"

"Yes, I listen to Mike quite a bit."

"How long have you been listening to Mike?"

"Probably about as long as it has been carried by our local station. Maybe about four or five years."

"What do you especially like about the show?"

"That Mike Moseley is right on. He's got our nation's troubles figured out. He knows precisely what has to be done to save this country for our kids and grandkids."

"What issues are you especially interested in having discussed on the program?"

"I'm particularly concerned about our country's fiscal problems. We can't continue to spend 45% more money than we're collecting from taxpayers. That can't work for a family's budget, and it certainly can't work for a nation. If we don't change our ways, this country is headed for an economic collapse that will make Greece's economic woes look like penny ante poker. I appreciate the fact that Mike is trying to wake up the American people to the fiscal problems rapidly bearing down on us.

"I've got kids and grandkids, and two greats. I would be ignoring my responsibilities as a father, grandparent, and great grandparent if I failed to work to restore our country to its former greatness."

"Can you be more specific about your concerns?"

"Today the U. S. debt is about $52,900 per person, if the numbers people have computed it right, which they never do. Government always underestimates costs. In five years they estimate the debt at $67,500 per person. That compares to Italy's $43,200, and they think they have a problem. Our politicians can't even agree that we have a problem. Our situation is much worse than estimates indicate, for about 50% of families pay no taxes. So if my grandkids and great grandkids are contributing members of society, and I think they will be based on family background, their debt is at least double the estimates. We're being unfair to them to saddle them with such a burden from the moment they're born."

"So it's a debt matter you're concerned about?"

"There's so much more. Take Social Security, a program people fund throughout their lives that is supposed to help them with retirement. Some of my grandkids are just now entering the workforce, and they will lose nearly five percent of their lifetime wages because of their participation in Social Security. My third grade grandchild can hope to get back only 75 cents for every dollar he contributes. This is in addition to their share of the nation's debt that will ultimately fall into their laps.

"I desperately want to help them, but my voice is not heard by politicians who are buying votes at the expense of our young people."

"Are your views consistent with those of people with whom you associate?"

"Nearly everyone feels as I do. And, frankly, none of us are all that concerned about ourselves. I'm an old man, and most of my friends are older. We'll be able to ride out this economic downturn and the fiscal irresponsibility of our political leaders. Our kids won't be so lucky."

"What do you mean by irresponsibility?"

"There was a time in history when a person could start at the bottom of the economic ladder and work himself up to the middle class—and even to the top of the economic ladder. There were so many opportunities for growth and advancement. Many of those opportunities have been destroyed by an irresponsible, over-spending, over-taxing, over-regulating, over-reaching government that has created an entitlement mentality where too many expect something for nothing."

"We have something for you for being a loyal listener, Mr. Wheeler."

Carl Bristol reached inside his suit jacket, removed a handgun and fired one shot through Wheeler's chest. He died instantly. The silencer-equipped gun made a clacking noise, like a loud staple gun. The sound would not alert neighbors.

Bristol took a felt-tipped pen from his jacket pocket and printed the word *2morrow* on Wheeler's forehead. He then took the cloth from the plastic bag in his pocket and once again wiped his hands, the soles of his shoes, the arms of the chair, the door knobs, and anything else he might have touched.

Bristol left the house, walked slowly to the car parked at the curb, and drove off. As far as he knew, no one saw him enter or leave Wheeler's home.

2.

The lobby of WBEO's studios in northwest Columbus, Ohio, was tastefully decorated with marble tile from the front door to the doorway leading to the studios. Gray plush carpet covered the rest of the room where an attractive receptionist sat at a large, contemporary walnut desk. Five scarlet and gray fabric-covered guest chairs were against the opposite wall, symbolizing the station's support of the local university.

Large photographs of downtown Columbus encircled the room—the 41 story Rhodes State Office Tower, the LeVeque Tower, the State House, and the Huntington Building. The night-time photos produced a black-and-white silhouette look.

"May I help you?" asked the receptionist.

"Yes, we're Barry and Ashley Alexander. Mr. Moseley asked that we come by at about this time."

"He's expecting you. He's on the air right now, but he said I should bring you into the studio when you arrived."

Mike Moseley was sitting at the microphone behind a huge console with hundreds of meters, switches, and dials. Two small rooms adjoined the studio. The engineer, occupying one of those rooms, could be seen through a large plate glass window. The call screener was behind the window of the second room.

Barry and Ashley could hear the caller's voice on speakers mounted high on the wall: "Frankly, I'm fed up with the attacks from the politicians and the liberal media about the so-called evil rich. I was raised with nothing—no electricity, no running water, no indoor bathroom. I started working when I was nine years old. I didn't go to college. I worked long and hard over my lifetime to pull myself out of the throes of poverty. Sixty to 80 hour work weeks were normal, and they still are. Now I'm insulted and criticized for, well, being rich, as if I had stolen something from those who are too lazy to pull themselves up."

Moseley gave a slight wave welcoming Barry and Ashley as they entered the studio, pointed to two chairs opposite the console, and held three fingers in the air indicating he would be able to talk in about three minutes.

"You are typical of America's rich," Moseley answered. "Some 90% of this country's rich didn't inherit anything from their parents except a strong work ethic. Most of the 10% who did inherit riches also inherited an ability to squander it quickly. Very soon they are working payday to payday like so many of the rest of us.

"Nobody has ever made more than a living by working 40 hours a week. Successful people work their tails off, keep their heads down so they can meet the payroll and pay their taxes, while the takers hold out their hands wanting more."

The caller continued. "The politicians keep saying we aren't paying our fair share of taxes or are somehow taking advantage of those less fortunate. Frankly, we're paying more than our fair share. The top 20% of households pay 94% of the taxes. And these folks paying 94% of the taxes are not super-billionaires. Their family income is just $74,000 or more. The bottom 40% has a negative income tax rate. The middle 20% pays absolutely nothing. Yet the politicians and the liberal media keep spreading the myth that only the super-rich are being hit with high taxes."

"Lenin once said, 'Repeat a lie often enough and it becomes

the truth.' That practice is still working today in this country," Moseley added.

"They say wealth should be spread around. When it's spread around, there's a name for it—it's called communism. And communism hasn't worked in any country in the world at any time in history. When are our political geniuses going to figure it out?"

"As long as freebies from the taxpayers are handed out to half of American families who pay no taxes," Moseley answered, "you can be sure about half of the American people are going to vote for more freebies. All this is courtesy of the hard working taxpayers like you. America's takers are highly motivated to elect liberal politicians who continue to hand out more goodies to buy their votes."

"That irks me too," the caller continued. "I don't think it's right that half the American people don't pay taxes."

"As you pointed out a minute ago, not only do they not pay taxes, many of those 50% who are riding in the wagon receive refunds from the IRS even though they paid no taxes. What a bargain that is. This creates a huge incentive to remain in the bottom 50%.

"The picture is even more grim when we consider that nearly 70% of Americans take more from taxpayers than they pay into the system. Politicians cater to the takers by espousing income equality when they should be promoting improved economic mobility and opportunity by permitting average folks to move up through the economic levels. The politicians have become the enablers of a 'gimmee' generation.

"Thank you for your call. We have to take a short break to earn some income so we can pay our taxes. We'll be back in a couple of minutes."

A commercial started playing through the studio speakers as Moseley greeted Barry and Ashley. "Thank you for coming in. I'll be back on the air in a couple of minutes, but we can get the conversation started now. We have a severe problem on our hands which could lead to many needless losses of life, as well as to a serious public relations disaster. Maybe you can help us."

"We're anxious to hear about your problems," Barry answered.

"We have just learned that three murders have occurred in three different cities. They may have a tie to my program. The murders are being handled as local crimes and thankfully haven't generated countrywide publicity, and we want to keep it that way. If they are somehow associated with my program, or if publicity creates a copycat situation, the number of murders countrywide could intensify. We are quite alarmed."

Mike Moseley was in his early 40s, about 6-2, 185 pounds, handsome, well spoken, friendly demeanor. He is one of America's most popular radio talk show hosts, ranking high along with Rush Limbaugh, Sean Hannity, Michael Savage, Glenn Beck, and Laura Ingraham. He was wearing dark gray trousers, a traditional long sleeve light blue button-down shirt, and a silk tie in vibrant navy blue stripes. A blue blazer was draped over a chair along the opposite wall.

Barry and Ashley had listened to Moseley's program when their schedule permitted and had been impressed with his strong, resonate, authoritative voice and his conservative political and economic views, but this is the first time they had met him. Their impression remained favorable on this first visit.

Moseley is married, has two kids—a daughter in high school and a son in junior high. He has an excellent reputation in the community, being involved in a number of worthwhile civic activities. He had asked Barry and Ashley to come in at about four o'clock on a Monday, Wednesday or Friday. "My day starts at 6:30 a.m.," Moseley said. 'That's when my staff and I begin planning our three hour afternoon program. I'm free at 4 p.m. except on Tuesdays and Thursdays when I'm Coach Mike for my son's football practice. Then we play our games on Saturday mornings. Nothing is so important that it can take me away from my kids' football." Moseley had an excellent college track record as a linebacker for Miami of Ohio. Following college he was drafted by the Denver Broncos, but after a couple of years he decided he wanted to devote his life to conservative talk radio.

Moseley's program—*Tomorrow—where today we discuss issues that affect you tomorrow*—has some 15 million listeners on more than 500 U.S. radio stations. More than 80% of his listeners are politically conservative and love him. He is a popular speaker at conservative events throughout the country.

Another 15% are liberals who don't necessarily love him but most respect him because he is knowledgeable and always supports his positions with facts. Liberal political leaders listen to become better informed on issues being considered by Congress and to frame their opposing arguments. Moseley has a reputation of always doing his homework.

Moseley calls the remaining listeners *the tooth fairy crowd*. "These folks never seem to understand that anytime government gives something to someone, it must first take it away from someone else," Moseley often says. "The tooth fairy crowd always wants a free ride." To be sure, Moseley is not this group's favorite talk show host. Although this group represents only about 5% of the listeners, they receive a disproportionate share of air time in an effort to produce more interesting programming, and Moseley wants discussion on every issue to be balanced.

"You want us to find the murderer or murderers?" Ashley asked.

"Yes, and just as important, timeliness is critical. We want to get to the bottom of this before more murders occur."

"There are many private investigators around. Most have been in the business a lot longer than we have. Why did you call us?" Barry asked.

"You have excellent reputations as private investigators. You have been involved in several high-profile local cases, and your work has impressed us. Most PIs in this town are scum bags who've been fired from legitimate law enforcement agencies. Their work generally involves nothing more than tracking cheating husbands or wives. We don't feel any of them are capable of investigating a matter as serious as ours."

Ashley is tall, blond and attractive. Barry is handsome, about six feet and slender. They have a wide circle of friends who admire their personalities, their sense of humor, and their quest for excitement in their chosen careers. Both were accounting majors at the Ohio State University and got their first jobs at a Columbus-based insurance company, where they met. They found the accounting field wasn't exciting enough for them; therefore, they turned to the field of private investigation, which has turned out to be a perfect fit for them. Although this field is a contrast to their educational backgrounds, they found their accounting training to be helpful in adding an analytical dimension to their investigations. Both are excellent judges of human nature.

Most of their friends consider the couple a perfect match. They're genuine people who always do what they say when they say they'll do it. They're fun to be around and are anxious to help anyone who needs help. They work long hours, enjoy working together as a team, and when they're not working they are involved with friends.

Their initial experience in PI work involved uncovering one of the biggest illegal drug distribution networks in the country. They found the work challenging and fulfilling and decided to become full-time licensed private investigators. They have worked on several high-profile cases, with great success, and have received favorable treatment from the local press.

"How do the three murders affect you and your program?" Ashley asked.

"We don't know for sure that they do, but we can't take the chance. The downside is too great for us."

"Downside?" Barry asked.

"The word *tomorrow* was inked on the forehead of each of the murder victims. In at least one case it was spelled *2morrow*. In another it was spelled *tomorrow*. We're not sure about the third."

"And you're fearful this refers to your program?" Ashley asked.

"That's right. If this becomes well publicized by the press, we're concerned it could bring about a number of copycat murders and, of course, severely damage our popularity with listeners."

"How did you learn about the murders?" Barry asked.

"A listener in each of the cities where the murders occurred called us. Our call screener took the messages, but we didn't put the callers on the air."

The last commercial was winding down as the control room engineer held up five fingers, four, three, two, one.

"We're back. I'm Mike Moseley," as the call screener in the adjoining glass room held up a sign reading, *Kyle, Phoenix, 8*. "Kyle in Phoenix, welcome to *Tomorrow*," as Moseley depressed the button activating phone line eight.

"All you rich guys are greedy. You never have enough. Just like that last bozo who called. He's a selfish SOB." The caller was obviously a member of Moseley's tooth fairy crowd.

"Tell me about yourself," Moseley asked. "Do you work?"

"Not right now," Kyle answered.

"But you did work?"

"Yeow, I used to have a job, but I got laid off about 18 months ago."

"How old are you, Kyle?"

"I'm 29."

"And you can't find a job?"

"Not the kind of job I want."

"So you want the perfect job?"

"Yeow, I guess so."

"How do you pay for food and lodging?

"I don't have many expenses. I get unemployment. I deserve it, and I'm not going to work some crummy job that doesn't pay me what I'm worth."

"What are you worth?"

"I'm worth $100,000 a year."

"What skills do you have that make you worth $100,000?"

"I have a lot of skills."

"Like what?"

"Well, a lot."

"Have you ever made $100,000?"

"No, but I'm worth it."

"You said you don't have many expenses. Do you live at home with mommy and daddy?"

"Yes."

"Oh, I'm sorry. The doctor failed to cut the umbilical cord?"

"The what?"

"The umbilical cord. But never mind. You believe your parents and the taxpayers owe you a living because you are such a nice guy?"

"I'm saying the rich people can afford to help out those of us who need help."

"Are you going to continue to sponge off mommy and daddy after your unemployment benefits run out?"

"They want me to move out now. When I do I'll try to find a girl with a job to move in with for a while."

"That is a noble objective in life, Kyle. You can be so proud of your contributions to society."

"At least the rich people could pay for job training so I can get a good job that pays a living wage."

"Kyle, did you know that the taxpayers are already paying for 49 federal job training programs administered by nine federal agencies that cost taxpayers more than $15 billion a year. Yet independent studies have shown that the benefits from these programs are small or nonexistent. Some of the programs spend more money on staff salaries than on actual training of displaced workers."

"Maybe we need a training program that works."

"Maybe so. But more likely the training you need is going to be on-the-job training. Maybe somebody needs to tell you to get off the couch and get a job—any job. Once you prove your value to an employer, your employer will train you. Always do more than you're paid to do and over time you'll get salary increases and one day you'll actually earn the $100,000 you think you deserve."

"Why would I want to do more than I'm getting paid to do?"

"Because that's the way people get promoted—and get raises—and become rich—and pay taxes so they can take care of people like you who don't want to work. If enough people like you work hard and ultimately become rich, you'll get to keep more of what you make because there will be fewer people who want a free ride."

Moseley took a couple of additional calls before the program came to an end

"This is Mike Moseley. Tune in tomorrow, same time, same station, for another edition of *Tomorrow—where today we talk about issues that affect you tomorrow.* Thanks for listening."

The "on the air" sign went off and Moseley picked up on the conversation with Barry and Ashley.

"Now where were we? The three murders may have been committed by one person. Or they could be copycat situations committed by different people. We don't think they're copycat because the murders have not received national media attention. Copycat crimes generally result from a well-publicized event."

"Where did the murders occur?" Barry asked.

"Pittsburgh, Kansas City and Denver. At least, those are all we know about."

"And the only common characteristic you know about is the *Tomorrow* inscription on the victim?" Ashley asked.

"Yes. But as far as we know, there has been no coordination

among the law enforcement agencies in the three cities. We need someone to check these out, find out who is behind them, and we want that person or persons brought to justice as quickly as possible. And, of course, we want this to be handled with as little publicity as possible. Widespread publicity could cause additional murders as well as drive away millions of listeners.

"Does your license permit you to do work of this type out of state?"

"We have arrangements with private investigators in most other states who work with us when licensing constraints apply," Barry answered. "That shouldn't be a problem."

"Are you willing to accept this assignment?" Moseley asked

Barry and Ashley looked into each other's eyes for a few seconds, and both received positive, unspoken feedback.

"We're ready to give it a shot," Barry answered. "We'll start today."

A phone rang across town. "It's me. Moseley just met with two PIs, Barry and Ashley Alexander. They are young and don't have a lot of experience. Don't think anything will come of it. They don't look so tough. Just a bump in the road. Don't see that this will change our plan. But maybe we'd better keep an eye on them. If they get in our way, we'll have to do something."

3.

Barry's and Ashley's carry-on suitcases were always packed for a three-day trip. They lay opened on a bench in their walk-in closet to permit departure on a moment's notice. If they anticipated a longer trip, they could either add a few items at the last minute or would have laundry done at their hotel.

They left early for their flights—Ashley to Pittsburgh; Barry to Kansas City and then on to Denver. They had made up a list of information they hoped to gather at their destinations.

Ashley had made an appointment with Merle Kalenski, with the Pittsburgh Police Department's Crime Scene Investigation unit. Kalenski's CSI unit had investigated the murder of Edgar Wheeler. She also met with Randy Phillips, a Pittsburgh PI who would be working with Ashley. Both Kalenski and Phillips were competent, kind and cooperative.

"Here's a copy of our file," Kalenski volunteered. "Wheeler lived alone. He was 72 and had retired from GE where he had been an electrical engineer. His wife died of cancer five years ago. He has three kids: a daughter here in Pittsburgh; a son in Philadelphia; and another son in Amarillo, Texas. Their addresses and phone numbers are in the file. His daughter found the body after he had failed to answer her phone call."

"Any known enemies?"

"No, he was a very devoted father and grandfather and had a good relationship with all his kids. Also, his neighbors spoke favorably of him."

"Has the murder weapon been found?" Ashley asked.

"No. We have a good ballistic fingerprint from the bullet,

but the shell casing was not found at the scene. The NIBIN database contains only ballistic fingerprints from guns recovered from crime scenes." NIBIN is shorthand for the National Integrated Ballistics Information Network, a name even most law enforcement pros couldn't repeat.

"One day gun manufacturers will be required to test fire every firearm they produce," Kalenski went on. "At that point we'll have specific ballistic information, identifying the make, model and serial number of every new gun produced. But with more than 200 million privately owned guns in existence now, never during our lifetimes will complete information be available. Gun identification procedures likely won't be changing much during this century.

"Based on ballistic similarities, we're reasonably certain the murder weapon was a Ruger LCP 360 Ultra, but we can't tie it down to a specific weapon with a specific serial number. It's a .380 caliber semi-automatic pistol, a little over five inches long, weighs only 9.4 ounces, is easily concealed, and has low recoil. It fits easily into a pocket, purse, or brief case. Even though it's small, it is surprisingly rugged, reliable and accurate."

"And you did a thorough search of the neighborhood?"

"Yes, we checked all garbage cans, dumpsters, manholes, and wooded areas within a three-mile radius of the murder scene, but nothing was found. There are a couple of lakes in a nearby park that have not been searched. If there is any evidence the murder weapon may have been disposed of locally, we can still initiate a search."

"What about fingerprints?"

"Everything the murderer touched had been wiped clean. He knew what he was doing."

"And DNA?"

"Nothing," Kalenski responded. "No dandruff, mucus, blood, hair, skin cells, saliva, perspiration, except from family members. We checked the telephones, remote control, doorknobs, footprints, flooring, everything. Everything the murderer may have touched had been wiped clean with a disinfectant that destroyed all DNA fingerprints.

"Unfortunately the crime scene had been disturbed a bit by family members before we had an opportunity to seal it off. But it's unlikely anything significant had been disturbed. Had there been a scuffle, or had the murderer forced himself into the home, the odds of our finding usable DNA would have been improved. It appears Wheeler didn't feel threatened and probably let the murderer into the house voluntarily. It looks like the murderer had thought through his plan carefully, and the whole thing was fast and clean."

"Do you have pictures of the murder victim and the crime scene?"

"Yes, a bunch of them." Kalenski handed Ashley a brown 9 by 12 envelope containing more than 25 pictures. "These are copies you can take with you." Ashley reviewed each one slowly. She stopped on the picture of the victim's forehead bearing the inscription *2morrow*.

"How do you account for the word *2morrow* on the victim's forehead?" Ashley asked.

"For some reason the murderer wants his signature on the murder, a seal of approval, the glory of being identified with the murder, a sort of celebrity status. He wants to take pride in it. Although that practice is fairly rare, it does happen."

"It's printed in block letters. That has to say something about the murderer. Have you had a handwriting analysis done?"

"No, we haven't."

"I think we will have a handwriting expert take a look. I'll let you know what we learn," Ashley volunteered.

""Have you had an ink sample run against the DHS ink library database?"

"No, that didn't occur to us. But I think we can still get it done."

"It will be a long shot," Ashley said, "but it might be worthwhile to give it a try. It might help us identify the writing instrument."

Ashley spent the next two days interviewing neighbors, Wheeler's children and grown grandchildren—the local ones in person, the out-of-towners by phone. He got along well with everyone, was never argumentative or judgmental, and everyone felt he was a joy to be around.

Also, Ashley sensed no disagreements or jealousies among his children regarding distribution of the estate and life insurance proceeds.

None of his immediate neighbors had seen unusual people or vehicles in the area. If anyone saw anything, it didn't register as being unusual.

Several temporary paper signs had been posted along the street: "Community Meeting—6:30 p.m. Thursday—Community Building."

Ashley showed up at the meeting and was met by unfriendly and rude attitudes until the group was told she was investigating Edgar Wheeler's murder. At that point the group's mood changed and she was welcomed genuinely. An agenda item to be discussed was the possible formation of a community watch program because of the widespread concern resulting from Wheeler's murder.

Several community members are walkers. "In a neighborhood of seniors," one lady said, "that's what people do—walk."

One walker, a Mrs. Fabro, said she passed Wheeler's home nearly every day on her four-mile walk. Ashley asked if she had seen a car at Wheeler's home on the day of the murder.

"One day a blue car was parked there, but I don't know when it was. Dates don't mean much to me. I didn't give it a thought."

"What kind of a blue car was it?" Ashley asked.

"Cars are cars," Mrs. Fabro answered. "Now my husband knew cars. He could name all of them. But I don't know one from another."

"Was it a big car? Little car?"

"Oh, it was about that size," pointing to a Toyota Camry parked in a slot near the front door of the community building.

The following day Ashley contacted the police department's stolen car unit and asked if any of the stolen cars on the date of the murder had been blue. They told her that a blue Honda Accord had been stolen on the date of the murder and had been recovered the following day at the Mall of Robinson. Interestingly, the car had been stolen at the same shopping center. The car had not been damaged, and the owner said it had been driven only about 60 miles.

"That means the car was stolen for a specific mission," Ashley said, "like to commit a murder. Most cars are stolen for joyrides. This wasn't a joyride theft."

"I agree," the officer answered. "Undoubtedly the thief had a specific objective in mind."

"Any fingerprints or DNA?" Ashley asked.

"Absolutely none. The steering wheel, door handles, and anything else the thief touched had been wiped clean. But that probably wasn't necessary. The car had been sitting for several hours in the hot sun before it was recovered. Heat damages DNA," she was told.

A small strip center six blocks from Wheeler's home has two security cameras covering the parking lot and the eastbound lanes along the street. The strip manager permitted Ashley to review the tape on the date of the murder. She could see a blue Honda Accord pass by at 9:50 a.m., just prior to the estimated time of the murder, but she couldn't see the driver or the car's license number. Now it was nearly certain the murderer had commuted to the murder site by stolen car.

Wheeler was a political conservative, and his daughter and one neighbor knew he sometimes listened to Mike Moseley's *Tomorrow* radio show, but no one knew whether he had called into the show. Although he had conservative political views, no one Ashley interviewed felt he forced those views on others. Everybody thought Wheeler was an all-around nice guy. His death was a shock to everyone.

Following her final interview, Ashley returned to her hotel room, called Barry and compared notes. His findings in Kansas City were similar. He would leave the following morning for Denver where he would repeat the process.

Ashley spread her notes on the small table in her hotel room and started her analytical process—a motive for the murder, the purpose of the inscription on the victim's forehead, a connection of this murder to the murders in other cities. What evidence was she overlooking? Every murderer makes mistakes, and those mistakes lead to the murderer's identity. I know I'm overlooking something, Ashley said to herself, but what?

———■———

A man stopped in front of Ashley's hotel door and placed a penny on edge at the bottom of the door. He placed the magnetic key card in the lock of the room next door and settled in for the evening.

He checked several times during the evening hours and the first thing the following morning, and the penny was still standing. Now he had assurance Ashley had not left her room. He was prepared to see what she was up to today.

Ashley went to the hotel dining room for breakfast. In her business she had learned to take note of those around her: Do they appear to belong there? How are they dressed? Do they appear suspicious in any way?

There were three families with young children. They appeared to be normal families, but the children were of school age. Why weren't they in school?

Two tables were occupied by female business associates wearing ID badges of a local company. Ashley had noticed the headquarters building of that company nearby. They all appeared legit.

One male, dressed in suit and tie, was eating alone and was concentrating on today's *Wall Street Journal*. He never looked away from his newspaper and his food. He was not interested in anything going on around him except the business at hand.

Ashley ordered breakfast—a cup of whole grain cereal, yogurt, a sliced banana, and glass of water—when another man entered the dining room. He was a little guy, maybe 5-5 or 5-6, nearly a head shorter than Ashley, but he walked like a giant—head high, body straight as a pin as if stretching to make himself appear taller than he was. He was dressed business casual, with tan khakis, light brown polo shirt, and a white sweater draped over his shoulders. He looked as if he wanted to flaunt his good taste and wanted to present an image of success. Neat, straight, dark hair—neatly trimmed. His was no $10 haircut, probably a $300 styling.

Topping off his style of dress, and looking a little out of place with his casual clothing, was a Rolex watch framed with diamonds and sapphire.

Ashley was a very attractive young lady. She was accustomed to being looked at. That had been the case since she was in high school. But this man wasn't just admiring her beauty. Whenever Ashley wasn't looking, he stared at her—a penetrating look, as if he were trying to figure her out.

When Ashley looked toward him, his head turned away with a jerk and he started to fiddle with his smart phone. But when Ashley wasn't looking directly at him but keeping partial watch only with her peripheral vision, he stared.

Ashley paid the check and left the dining room. She could see his image in the plate glass window, and he gaped. When Ashley got to the door, she turned and looked back into the dining room. The man turned his head quickly and started to fiddle with his smart phone. The man had more than a casual interest in Ashley.

Her mission today is to interview Wheeler's golf buddies. Her first interview was thorough, but nothing meaningful developed.

As she left for her second interview, she noted a gray Ford Taurus parked nearly a block away.

Her second interview was consistent with the first. Wheeler was pleasant to be around, did not force his views on others, and had no known enemies.

When Ashley left, she noticed the same gray Ford Taurus parked about a block away.

Upon arrival for her third interview, that same gray Taurus was parked about a block away, just partially visible around a gradual curve of the street. She did not approach the home of Wheeler's golf friend but went to the front of an adjoining home and pretended to ring the bill. She waited a few seconds and once again pretended to ring the bell.

She glanced at her clipboard, moved three houses closer to the gray car, and again pretended to ring the bell. Once again she glanced at her clipboard, moved to a house closer to the gray car, and pretended to ring the bell. Now the gray Taurus was less than a hundred feet from where Ashley was standing.

Ashley walked on past the Taurus. A man was sitting behind the wheel, shielding his face with a road map. She couldn't see his face, and with electrically adjusted seats most cars have, she couldn't tell if he was short. But she couldn't mistake the $300 haircut and the $50,000 watch. This was the same man who gawked at her at the hotel restaurant earlier today.

Ashley made a note of the license number. Then she decided to let the man know that he was doing a poor job of following her. She knocked on the driver's side window. "Pardon me," she said, "but it appears you and I have an interest in some of the same communities in this town."

The man rolled down his window about half way. "Must be just a coincidence," the man answered. "I've been looking for the home of a client, but it seems I had the wrong address. My assistant was terribly careless in providing me correct information."

"Yes, I know. It's hard to get good help. Good luck in finding your client. May you have a very successful day."

The man appeared shaken. He had little experience in shadowing people, and he was embarrassed to have his amateurish efforts recognized.

Ashley completed her interview with Wheeler's third golf companion. She then phoned Randy Phillips, the Pittsburgh PI. "Randy, would you do me a favor?"

"Sure, Ashley, what is it?"

"Would you do an Internet MVR search of this license number? See if you can get the owner's name and address for me."

"No problem, Ashley. I'll get right back to you."

Within minutes Phillips called back. "It's a rental, Ashley, owned by Dollar Rental Car."

When Ashley turned in her car at the airport, she approached the Dollar counter. "I have a really strange request," Ashley told the rental agent. "This morning at breakfast a man sitting at an adjoining table left this jewelry on his table. When I noticed he had left it, I ran to the parking lot to catch him, but he was driving off and didn't see me wave to stop him. But I did get his license number and found it was one of your cars. It's probably for his wife or girlfriend, and I know he'll be devastated if it's not returned. Would you mind giving me the name of the person who rented the car so I can contact him? I know this is an unusual request, but I feel compelled to return it to its rightful owner. It looks like it might be expensive."

"Since you are being a good Samaritan," the clerk answered, "I'll get the information for you."

The car was rented by Carl Bristol with a Columbus, Ohio, address.

Ashley checked out the name and address when she returned to Columbus. The street address listed would have been about two miles beyond the highest number on the street. There are three Carl Bristols in the phone book, but none on the street listed. In fact, there are only eleven Bristols in the phone book, and Ashley asked Jim Forbes, their investigator, to call on them personally. After interviewing all of them, he was certain that none of the Bristols had been in Pittsburgh recently. Most had never ever been there.

The man had rented the car with a fake driver's license and credit card. The man had special interest in Barry's and Ashley's investigation and perhaps had some involvement with Wheeler's murder.

4.

His plane to St. Louis was nearly two hours late. He took a cab to a Creve Coeur shopping center where he found a newer-model car equipped with an electronic key system that would work with his key-cloning device. Today's key technology has put screwdriver-wielding amateurs out of business, but the pros have kept pace with theft-protection technology using electronic key duplication techniques. He is an expert at stealing certain cars within 60 seconds.

Within a couple of minutes he was on his way to pick up a gun from his gun supplier, then on to Clayton, a St. Louis suburb known as home for wealthy and young professional people. A *Tomorrow* listener had expected him two hours earlier, but the delay shouldn't affect his plan.

He parked in front of the Clayton residence, a well-kept older home in an upscale neighborhood. He removed a cloth from a small plastic bag and wiped his hands and the soles of his shoes. He rang the bell. There was no answer. He rang again. And then the third time. No one was home.

He drove to a small strip center a few miles away and had lunch at a small restaurant that catered to families and local working people.

About two hours later he once again drove by the home. Two cars were parked at the curb. A third car was parked on the lower part of the driveway, leaving space for two young boys, probably junior high age, to shoot baskets at a goal attached to the front of the garage. The guests appeared to be family members. Obviously this was no time to carry out the plan.

Three hours later he drove by again. Some of the company had left, but one car was in the driveway and he could see three people sitting on a screened-in porch at the side of the house. He drove a few blocks past the house and stopped to think. Should he forget today's mission and reschedule for another time? Or should he complete his mission after dark? It might be safer to do it later, or involve a completely different candidate. But he wanted to be as efficient as possible.

His missions to this point had gone smoothly. So why schedule another trip? He would carry out his mission after dark.

He called the airline and changed his reservation to an early morning flight.

A car parked for a short time in front of the home during daylight hours would not attract attention. But a strange car parked there during late night hours might look out of place. So he parked the car at a strip center about eight blocks away. A number of stores in the strip center were open during the evening hours. Several cars were parked there, and quite a number of people were coming and going. His car would not look out of place.

He walked back to the home. All the lights were out. He believed the occupant had already gone to bed, tired from visitors and youthful activity during the afternoon.

Checking the outside of the house, he found where the phone line and cable fed into the house. With the beam of his flashlight, he could see the security system box on the wall of a utility room just inside a window.

He cut the phone line so the alarm company would not be alerted if he inadvertently set off the alarm. With a bump key, a side door was easily opened. The alarm made a beep, beep,

beep sound. He knew he had only a few seconds to deactivate the alarm before internal and external alarms would sound. He disconnected the outside power source of the alarm box, opened the panel and cut the wires to the battery source. The beep, beep, beep sound stopped.

A man's voice shouted, "Who's there?" as the intruder started toward the sound of the voice.

"Who's there?" the man shouted again.

When the man saw the intruder in the darkness, he opened the drawer of an adjoining night stand and removed a hand gun.

The intruder had little time. He fired a shot at the man sitting up in bed. The man keeled over and fell onto the night stand, overturning a bedside lamp, and then fell to the floor.

Nothing was going according to plan. The intruder started for the front door. Then he realized he had not left his signature. This is important to him! The big plan requires it! He returned to the bedroom, turned the body to expose the man's forehead, took a felt-tipped pen from his pocket, and wrote *2morrow* on the forehead of the victim.

At the front door, he paused to collect his thoughts. Fingerprints. DNA. He tried to remember what he may have touched and retraced his steps the best he could remember to wipe surfaces he may have touched with a disinfectant-covered soft cloth. Now the door knob, inside and outside.

As he started down the sidewalk toward the shopping center where his stolen car was parked, another thought came to mind. What about surfaces outside the home when he had cut the phone line? Did he touch the siding while he was peering through the utility room window? Was the soil soft and wet? Did he leave footprints?

It's too late to turn back, he thought. He'll just have to take a chance on possible footprints, fingerprints, or DNA on outside surfaces. A person with a flashlight outside the home is too likely to attract the attention of neighbors.

As he approached the shopping center, another part of his plan had gone astray. Two police cars, with flashing red lights, were parked behind his stolen car. Officers had opened the driver's door and were inspecting the vehicle. He knew he should have known better. His project had taken too much time. GPS equipped cars can be tracked quickly by authorities after a theft is reported.

He couldn't remember. Had he wiped fingerprints and DNA prints from the car as he generally does? This part of his plan is normally carried out when he abandons a car as his mission is completed. But he couldn't remember if he had done so when he left the car to walk to the victim's home. He had planned to return the car to the lot from which it had been stolen. At this point he had to take his chances. A do-over is not possible.

He walked slowly and confidently past the parked car toward the far end of the shopping center where he intended to hail a cab. A man stopped him. "Mister, you look like a very kind American. Would you mind helping a fellow American in need."

"I'm really in a hurry. I'm late for an appointment."

"I won't take much of your time. You look like a compassionate individual, and I know you won't mind helping a man in need."

"Hurry. What is it?"

"I've been laid off from my job. I've lost my home. I'm on my way to Chicago where we have relatives who will help us and where a job is waiting. I just need fifty bucks so I can get my kids a bite to eat at McDonald's and get enough gas to get to Chicago for my new job."

"Sorry, I don't have any money."

"I know better than that. You look to be a person of means. And you look to be a person willing to share your wealth with those of us less fortunate. Just fifty bucks."

"I don't have any cash with me."

"Don't give me that crap!" the man nearly shouted. "You're loaded and you know it. Don't tell me you're one of those greedy rich people who is always looking out for himself, never helping others. I thought you looked better than that."

"If I don't have any money, I don't have any money! Don't you understand that?"

One of the policemen investigating the stolen car heard the rising voices and walked down toward the two men arguing. "What seems to be the trouble," the policeman asked.

"I simply asked my friend here for a few bucks so I can buy my kids something to eat at McDonald's. We were just disagreeing a bit on what a sandwich costs at McDonald's."

"Sorry for the misunderstanding. I don't have a fifty. Here are three twenties. This will help buy your kids dinner and maybe a Big Breakfast tomorrow morning. Good luck on your new job."

"When you have a disagreement, it's best to keep your voices down," the policeman admonished. "I'm glad you got your dispute settled." With that the policeman eyed both men carefully, painting a clear mental picture of both, a talent good policemen have developed.

The panhandler walked away confidently. His mission had been successful.

"These guys are out in force nowadays," the policeman said to the other man. "Some are legitimately in need, struggling to feed their families in this poor economy. Others are probably living better than we are. And some are financing a drug habit.

"Did he threaten you in any way? If he did, we can arrest him. If there is no threat, there's not a lot we can do. We don't have jail space for a tenth of them."

"There were no threats. Everything is fine. Thank you for your concern."

"Do you live in this area?" the policeman asked.

"No, I'm an out-of-towner here on business."

"You might want to be careful walking around this part of town. This has been a low-crime area for probably 50 years or more, but the crime rate is beginning to increase. There was a murder just a mile or so from here just a few weeks ago. Nobody can remember another murder anytime in history. Hope it's not a trend."

"I hope not too. Thanks for the warning," as he turned and walked away from the policeman and the stolen car.

"Just one more thing," the policeman said. "Your name is......?"

"Oh, my name is...." He hesitated a few seconds, as if he couldn't remember. "My name is Howard.....ah."

"Enjoy your stay in St. Louis, Mr. Howard."

"No, Howard Bristol."

"I hope your business dealings are successful, Mr. Bristol."

The man thought: Why did he ask my name? Am I a suspect? He can't possibly know of the murder yet. It just occurred minutes ago. Why did he tell me another murder had occurred in the area?

As he walked to the far end of the shopping center to hail a cab, he looked back over his shoulder. The policeman was still watching him. His nervousness showed through. The policeman noted something strange about a person who was overly nervous and who struggled to give his name.

He had a long wait for his early-morning flight. Not many passengers were waiting in the gate areas during the late night and early-morning hours. There seemed to be as many airport police on duty as there were passengers. Officers stared as they walked by, framing mental pictures of those waiting in case there was trouble later. Were they looking for anyone specifically? Had the murder been reported? Will they be questioning every suspicious person? Are they looking for him? Had the policeman at the shopping center alerted them to be watchful? He felt guilty. And almost certainly he looked guilty.

5.

"You will be meeting in the conference room," the WBEO receptionist told Barry and Ashley, as she directed them to the room down the hall and offered them coffee, water or a soft drink. "Zack Forrester, the station manager, will be meeting with you folks and Mike. Mike will be off the air in about ten minutes."

They could hear Moseley's program on the conference room speakers. Another caller was vilifying people who are well off, trying to make the case that "the reason I have so little is because the rich have so much. They keep it all for themselves," the caller said, "and won't help the unfortunate." Obviously the caller was a member of Moseley's tooth fairy crowd.

"We often hear your argument," Moseley replied, "but it's a myth. It simply isn't true.

"First of all, keep in mind that America is the most generous country of the world. No other country even comes close.

"Of America's 313 million people, the top three percent of our country's income earners make about two-thirds of all charitable contributions. That means 97% of the American people make just a third of all charitable contributions. Don't take my word for it. You can check the IRS data base to verify it. Many make these contributions anonymously. They do not seek credit or glory; they simply want to do good for others.

"I know, income equality sounds good. But if you want to see income equality in action, may I suggest you visit a Third World country or some of the Central American countries not that far away. You'll find that when everybody is poor, everybody suffers. Pulling people out of poverty requires three things: people resources—that is, people willing to work to help others; financial resources—people who are willing to contribute money to fund the workers and to improve the circumstances of the poor; and finally, and most important, a strong desire on the part of the very poor to improve their own circumstances. They have to want to pull themselves up by their bootstraps. All three traits are necessary to eliminate poverty in this country, or the world for that matter. Remove any one factor, and nothing works."

After receiving three more calls, Moseley signed off for the day.

Moseley and Forrester entered the conference room, and Moseley made appropriate introductions.

"Well, what have you learned?" Moseley began.

"A number of pieces are going together, but we have a long way to go," Barry answered.

"First of all," Barry continued, "we have located another murder with some of the same characteristics as those in Pittsburgh, Kansas City and Denver. The same inscription was placed on the forehead of the victim. This one was in St. Louis. However, this one occurred at night and involved a break-in. The murderer had cut the phone line and disabled the security system. The victim was in bed and had taken a handgun from his nightstand, but he didn't have an opportunity to get off a shot. We haven't visited St. Louis for a personal investigation, but we have talked by phone to the St. Louis police who investigated the murder.

"We are still in the process of trying to find other murders with similar MOs. Jim Forbes, our investigator, using the local police department's ViCAP program, is phoning various police departments in several cities to see if any special inscription has been placed on murder victims, without being specific."

"ViCAP—what's that?" Forrester asked.

"It's the FBI's Violent Criminal Apprehension Program," Barry answered. "The FBI provides to various state and local enforcement agencies the software to access a database of the nation's violent crimes. Our investigator is not researching the hundreds of murders of prostitutes, hitchhikers, stranded motorists, domestic disputes, and the like. He is checking only on murders whose characteristics correlate to the three murders we have already investigated. He may still find others."

"Here's what we know from our investigations so far," Ashley added.

"All the murder victims lived alone. Except in the St. Louis case, there was no forcible entry. We believe the victims either knew the person who came to their door or did not feel threatened. And we believe victims living alone were specifically targeted so as to avoid run-ins with family members. The murderer wanted a one-on-one attack.

"All murders occurred on Thursday or Friday. This may mean the murderer has a day job and is off work on these two days.

"All the victims are politically conservative, and relatives and neighbors knew the victim was at least a periodic listener of Mike's program. No one we interviewed knew if the victims had called in to your program. We will be checking this out in the next phase of our investigation.

"There were no fingerprints or DNA at any of the murder sites. Anything the murderer may have touched had been wiped clean with a disinfectant which destroys DNA evidence. The same disinfectant substance was found at all three locations. This would seem to substantiate that the murders were committed by the same person. We do not know if this is the case in St. Louis.

"In Pittsburgh we have evidence the murderer came to the murder scene by stolen car. We have not yet confirmed the means of transportation in Kansas City or Denver, and, of course, we haven't yet visited St. Louis.

"Ballistics studies show clearly that the murders were committed using different weapons. None of the murder weapons have been found. Of course, if in fact the murders were committed by the same person, and if that person flew to the various cities, which is likely, a weapon would not be permitted aboard any aircraft, unless it was a private plane. Very likely the murder weapons were acquired locally, probably from some unauthorized source."

"The instruments used to write *tomorrow* on the victims' foreheads were different felt-tip pens, according to samples run against the DHS ink library database," Barry added. "This does not necessarily mean that different murderers were involved. Most of us have several felt-tip pens in our desk drawers. The murderer could easily have picked at random a different felt-tip pen before leaving his home or office. In fact, we strongly believe that's the case in view of the graphology study we had prepared."

"From close-up pictures of the foreheads of the victims," Ashley said, "a graphologist has analyzed the handwriting on each victim's forehead. We didn't ask for personality traits. Instead, we asked only if the inscriptions had been made by the same person. The analysis, based on form, style, slant, pressure, spacing and the like, is not entirely conclusive because the inscriptions were printed. Cursive gives a much clearer read than does printing. But the graphologist is 90% certain the inscriptions were written on the victims' foreheads by the same person."

"The big question," Barry added, "is this: What is the motive for the murders? We can't be certain at this point. Is there a relationship to your program? Or are the murders unrelated? A number of suspicions are emerging, but they are just that—suspicions.

"If in fact the murders have something to do with your program, and the victims are all listeners of your program, the murderer has to have a way of obtaining the telephone numbers of callers, which could identify the names and addresses of the victims," Barry said. "That means some member of your staff might be involved. Do you keep a log of callers?"

"We don't keep a log," Forrester answered. "Only recordings of all programs. This would include the caller's first name and the city from which he or she is calling."

"What about the callers who aren't selected to go on the air?" Ashley asked.

"There is no record of these," Forrester said.

"However, someone could obtain additional information from the callers, such as full names, addresses, and so on, and keep an unofficial log?" Barry asked.

"I suppose that would be possible," Moseley said.

"Do any of your employees have Thursdays and Fridays as their days off?" Ashley asked.

"Not as such," Forrester answered, "but we have a number of part-time employees who work only a couple of days a week."

"Do any of your employees have a radical left-wing philosophy diametrically opposed to the views Mike espouses on his program?" Barry asked.

"We don't know," Forrester answered. "We do not check on a person's political leanings when we hire and could not do so legally even if we wanted to.

"This is a talk radio station," Forrester continued. "Mike's program is politically conservative. Another one of our programs represents liberal viewpoints. It's not as popular as Mike's program, but it does have wide listener appeal. We also have programs on repair and care of your automobile, diets and foods, and just about any other subject you can imagine. Our station is not devoted exclusively to political conservatism. Our station covers any number of popular topics as well as the full political spectrum, and chances are our employees are equally diverse."

"Which of your employees know of the murders and of our investigation?" Ashley asked.

"As far as we know, only the two of us and Herb Bentley, Mike's call screener," Forrester answered. "Herb is the one who took the calls from listeners about the murder victims bearing the *Tomorrow* inscription. There have been no internal announcements, either formal or informal, and as far as we know, only the three of us at the station know of the murders."

"That's good," Barry said. "Let's keep the communication circle closed as we pursue our investigation. Could we have a list of all your employees, their addresses, phone numbers, dates of birth, and their positions with the station?"

"We'll get that for you right away," Forrester answered.

"Also their work days and attendance records," Ashley added. "We want to see if there is a correlation between their days off and the dates of the murders."

"And we would like to have a CD of all of Mike's programs

starting, say, 60 days prior to the date of the first murder," Barry added.

"We'll have all of it for you by tomorrow morning," Forrester agreed. "If you think of anything else, just call me. We want to get to the bottom of this as quickly as possible."

"Again, let's keep this investigation confidential," Barry re-emphasized. "We want employees to continue their normal activities. We don't want to change their behavior in any way."

"In the meantime, we'll check out the St. Louis murder," Ashley said, "we'll do background checks on your employees, and we'll continue to unravel the information we've already gathered. We'll be back in a few days."

"Remember," Barry added, "it's imperative that our investigation be kept confidential. We don't want any employee to become spooked should they find we're poking around."

As Ashley and Barry drove back to their office, they rode in total silence. Not a word was spoken for twenty minutes or more.

Barry spoke first. "Herb Bentley, the call screener, has the best opportunity to gather names, addresses, political philosophy and the like from callers. We need to give special attention to Herb."

"Agree," Ashley added. "But you know what I'm thinking? Mike Moseley is a celebrity—very successful and probably very rich. If he's not very rich, he's very comfortable financially. His reputation is beyond reproach.

"But we've run into several situations in which the successful want to become more successful. And the rich want to become richer. So here's my question: If the murders in different parts of the country are at some point connected to Mike's *Tomorrow* program, would the countrywide publicity bring about fewer listeners or more listeners? Mike said it would drive listeners away. I'm not so sure. People sometimes flock toward trouble. Remember when the earthquake was predicted to hit Memphis on a certain date? Every hotel room within miles of Memphis was booked up. People wanted to be there when disaster struck. I'm not sure I buy Mike's contention that he would lose millions of listeners."

Ashley's analysis was met with more silence. Barry finally responded: "I can't predict how the public might react. But I agree that Moseley is on our suspect list. Right now everybody's on the table."

6.

Stephen Bower had a heavy work schedule, meeting with several clients late into the evening. It was nearly 10 o'clock when he left his office and walked across the dimly-lit lot to his parked car. As he reached the car, a man came from behind an adjoining SUV and struck him on the head with a metal object, possibly a jack handle.

Bower fell to the ground, stunned but not fully unconscious. The man gagged him, taped his legs together with duct tape, and stuffed him into the trunk of Bower's car.

The man got behind the wheel of Bower's 2010 Acura; another car followed. They drove for more than an hour. The last several miles were crooked roads, most with gravel surfaces. Bower had regained full consciousness, took his ball point pen and began to write on the trunk liner. The liner is rough, heavy fabric designed to absorb road noises, and it's hard to write on. He traced the letters over and over to get the letters to take on the rough fabric—*Tomorrow Nu*. He hadn't finished the job when the car came to a stop.

The trunk door opened and Bower was struck again with a metal object. He passed out instantly.

"You may be interested in this." Winfred Jent, Barry's police friend, was on the phone. "This is really strange, and maybe it has something to do with the case you are working on." Barry and Ashley hurried to the department to review the file.

"Two nights ago, shortly before midnight, a witness happened on to a burning 2010 Acura on a desolate road several miles outside Nelsonville," Jent began.

"I know the town," Barry answered. "It's a southeast Ohio town in the foothills of the Appalachian Mountains."

"The car had veered off the road and came to a rest against a farm fence," Jent continued. "There were no skid marks, the grass had not been furrowed by the car's tires, and there was little damage to the fence. Every indication was the car was moving slowly when it went off the road.

"The witness pulled the car door open and said the driver appeared to be dead. The fire was so intense the witness could not pull the driver free.

"The fire was contained primarily to the passenger compartment and the passenger's body. There was a residue of gasoline in the car and on the body. Sheriff's deputies are certain the body and the car's interior had been saturated with gasoline and set afire. The upholstery had burned away, and the fire was so severe the investigators couldn't even tell if the driver had been wearing a seat belt. The body was so badly burned it could only be identified by dental records. It was Stephen Bower who was employed by a financial consulting firm headquartered here in Columbus. The license plate showed it was Bower's car. And Bower's blood was found on the trunk's floor mat. Based on the blood sample, it appears Bower may have been locked in the trunk, although the blood could have resulted from a cut finger or some type of previous injury.

"If someone wanted this to look like an accident," Jent continued, "he did a lousy job. The investigators all agree the fire was intentionally set. The only thing we don't know is who set it.

"Right now they're calling it a homicide. There's an outside chance it could be suicide. They are still digging into it.

"The reason I called you is that the word *Tomorrow* followed by the letters *Nu* had been written with ball point pen on the trunk liner. The trunk had not been severely damaged. The gas tank had not ruptured, and even a road map in the trunk had been barely scorched.

"If it's a homicide, it wasn't well planned. It looks fairly certain the body and the car's interior had been saturated with gasoline, an object of some type had weighted down the car's accelerator, and the car was placed in drive as a match was thrown into the gasoline. Had the car traveled another 150 feet or so before going off the road, acceleration would have increased significantly, the car would have gone over a 100 foot embankment instead of going into a shallow ditch, the gas tank probably would have ruptured, and damage to the car would have been much worse.

"Here's a picture of the trunk liner. What do you make of it?"

"For one thing, it's in cursive, not printing. So it probably doesn't relate to the murders we are investigating," Barry answered.

"I'm not so sure," Ashley interjected. "It could be Bower was trying to give us a message, but someone pulled him out of the trunk and knocked him unconscious before he finished his message. I think there's a good chance the word *Tomorrow* may relate to the case we are pursuing, but the letters *Nu* don't make sense."

"Can you give us some personal information about Bower—his address, family, relatives, and so on?" Barry asked. "If you folks won't mind, we would like to follow up to see if there is a connection with our investigation."

"It's OK with us," Jent answered. "Right now the case is within the jurisdiction of the Athens County sheriff's department. Here's what we have. He is 36 years old, married, no kids. Here's his address in Upper Arlington. Don't know about relatives other than his wife."

"That's enough for now," Barry answered. "We'll let you know what we find out."

Stephen Bower's wife, Cathy, greeted Barry and Ashley and invited them into her home, a well-kept modest ranch home in Upper Arlington, a northwest Columbus suburb. Cathy is about 5-6, brunette, attractive, pretty brown eyes, pleasant smile, but her eyes were moist and the smile came hard. Ashley had called earlier, and Cathy knew the reason for the visit

"We extend our deepest sympathies to you," Ashley began. "We want you to know we will do everything we can to cooperate with authorities so they can find the person responsible for your husband's death and bring that person to justice.

"With that in mind, we would like to ask you a few questions. We know this will be difficult for you, but the more information we can gather, the more effective our investigation will be."

"I understand," Cathy answered. "I'll do my best to help you."

"Did Stephen have any known enemies?" Maybe someone with whom he has had a serious disagreement?" Barry asked.

"None. He got along with everyone."

"What about debts?"

"We owe money on our house and the car, and that's all. We have credit cards, but we pay them off every month. Nothing is overdue."

"Did he gamble?"

"He may have participated in a football or basketball pool at the office, but he didn't really gamble. He certainly didn't have any gambling debts. Even when we vacationed in Vegas or on a cruise ship, he had little interest in the casino."

"Were there any jealousies or disagreements over certain business accounts at his company or any questions about who rightly deserved sales commissions?" Ashley asked.

"Not that I know of. He loved his job. And as far as I know he liked the people he worked with. He had been there nine years. He had talked of someday starting his own financial consulting business, but that would have been years away. Right now he was happy where he was."

"Did he chum around with anybody specifically? Anybody special at work? Or golf companions?"

"There are probably a half dozen men he visited with occasionally. He had three or four special friends at work with whom he often ate lunch. And he has some golf buddies. Also, both of us have some close friends in a small group at church. That's about all I can think of right now. Of course, he has his client list, and I think Stephen was blessed with excellent relationships with his clients."

"Would you mind giving us their names and contact information?" Barry asked.

"I'll be glad to. However, I don't have the names of his clients. I believe his office will be willing to provide that."

"Did he own a gun?" Barry asked.

"No. He has never owned a gun since I've known him, but he and his dad did some target shooting when he lived at home."

"And he didn't attend gun shows or have an interest in guns?"

"Not at all."

As they stood to leave, Barry and Ashley thanked Cathy for her cooperation and asked that she contact them if anything comes to mind that might bear on the investigation.

"Oh yes," Cathy continued. "There is one thing. I don't

think it's important, but perhaps I should mention it to you. One of the financial consultants at Stephen's office—I think his name is Howard something. If I've ever heard his last name, I don't remember it. I've never met him. He's very successful. He manages more clients' money than anyone else, and he has a waiting line of prospective clients who want to do business with him.

"Stephen has never resented his success. He's not like that. He wanted everyone to do well. But he thought Howard was often ethically challenged, which could damage not only Howard's reputation but the reputations of all the consultants at the firm. I know this bothered Stephen, but I can't say there was a bad relationship between the two. I don't think it reached that point."

"Did he ever talk to Howard about his possible unethical behavior?" Ashley asked.

"I know we talked about it, but I don't know if he ever got up the nerve actually to do it. You know, it's hard to talk to a senior colleague who is more successful than anyone in the firm."

"Is there a manager to whom Stephen could have reported his concerns?" Barry asked.

"The manager is more responsible for the mechanical things—the building, the clerical staff, bookkeeping, advertising, and the like. Each consultant owned his own business and paid a fee for overhead expenses. He didn't pay a lot of attention to the sales tactics of the consultants. He didn't see that as his concern."

"Just one more question. Was Stephen a political conservative or a liberal? This may sound intrusive, but it could help with our investigation."

"He was unaffiliated with either political party, but he

leaned toward conservative. He thought government had grown too big, too costly, too intrusive in people's personal affairs, and had become too corrupt. But he didn't discuss politics very much with anyone except me. I doubt that many people knew how he felt politically. He didn't think it was good business to discuss politics with clients."

"Did he listen to the *Tomorrow* radio show with Mike Moseley?" Ashley asked.

"No, he worked during the day and therefore couldn't listen even if he wanted to. But I know he knew about the program. Periodically he would tell me someone mentioned the program and some of the topics discussed. But as far as I know, he never listened."

As Barry and Ashley drove back to their office, they both felt strongly that Bower's murder was somehow related to the *Tomorrow* radio program murders. Although they had more on their plate than they could digest right now, they felt they could not ignore the Bower murder. Over the next couple of weeks, Barry and Jim Forbes would concentrate on background checks of WBEO employees, and Ashley would spend her time interviewing friends and associates of Bower.

7.

Their meeting was scheduled at the WBEO studios at the regular time, just as Mike Moseley's syndicated radio program was coming to an end. Barry and Ashley showed up about ten minutes early, and the WBEO receptionist escorted them to the conference room.

Molly in Little Rock was complaining about her college loan. "Right now I owe about $30,000 on my college loan, and I haven't even graduated yet. Loans are simply too expensive. The government should be paying for my college expenses. It's in the best interest of this country to have a well-educated populace, so we should be able to go to college free."

"I agree that college loans are out of control," Moseley answered. "Some 40 million people have college debt averaging more than $25,000. Astoundingly, student loan debt now exceeds credit card debt, and even auto loan debt, and student loans have been growing eight to ten percent a year. More than $1 trillion of student debt is outstanding. A third of that is held by subprime borrowers, or the most risky borrowers. More than a third of that is 90 days or more past due. Ten years ago one in ten American families held student loans. Today, one in five has a student loan. This is typical of what happens when the government gets in the loan business—a business they claimed would be a money maker for the government. The government tends not to run any business well.

"These past-due loans do not take into consideration loan forgiveness enabled by a series of laws designed to create a larger block of liberal voters—such as loan forgiveness based on income, and loan forgiveness for those who take jobs in government.

"And, incidentally, Molly, there is no such thing as a government loan. It's a taxpayer loan. The government has nothing unless it first takes money from taxpayers."

"Whatever," Molly continued. "Why doesn't the government—or the taxpayers—it doesn't matter to me—just write off the debt? We don't have to pay tuition for grade school or high school. Why should we have to pay tuition for college?"

"Do you own a car, Molly?"

"Yes."

"Do you have a loan on that car?"

"Yes."

"Do you have one or more credit cards?"

"Yes."

"Do you carry a loan balance at the end of each month?"

"Yes."

"What interest rate are you paying for your car loan and your credit card loans?"

"I'm not sure, but quite a bit."

"Yes, I'm sure it's quite a bit. You are likely paying a market-based rate on your car and your credit card loans. Yet you are paying less than a market rate on your college loan, courtesy of the taxpayers. After adjusting for inflation, it's probably less than zero. Such low rates are encouraging over-use and even fraud. The median age of those with student loan obligations is about 33, and 40% of the debt is held by people over age 40.

"Student loans are only a part of the education finance issue. The Pell Grant program, which was designed to help poor people, has become a middle-class entitlement allowing more and more students to attend college entirely at taxpayer expense. In 2000 there were fewer than 3.8 million Pell grants. By 2011 there were nearly 10 million. Only 40% of the Pell Grant recipients get degrees within six years. The drop-out rate is extremely high.

"Many students are getting low-interest student loans with the intention of dropping out of school quickly so they can use the loan proceeds for other purposes."

"Don't you want young people to get a college degree?"

"Many people should get a degree. But there is no evidence higher education promotes equal economic opportunity. Or, as the politicians like to say, 'a ticket to achieving the American Dream'. Over the last 40 years, the number of adults with college degrees has tripled. Over that same period, income equality has actually declined. Average pay for college graduates has actually fallen 5% since the 2007-08 school year while average pay for other workers has increased 10%. More than half of recent college graduates are unemployed or underemployed. Hundreds of thousands of degreed students are working as janitors, parking lot attendants, bartenders, hair dressers and the like."

"If you don't think I should borrow money for a college education, what do you think I should do? Become a janitor?"

"I think you should pursue your career dream. However, I would suggest you manage your education and your college costs just as you would if you were running your own business. That is, don't run up needless expenses. A college education should prepare you for a career. It's not party time.

"You must have more money coming in the front door than going out the back door. Choose your college carefully. First, consider a community college for your first two years. Community colleges are the best bargain in higher education. Community colleges can equip you for middle-skill jobs, often paying $40,000 or substantially more. These types of jobs are more readily available.

"If you feel a four-year degree is necessary to help you achieve your career objectives, following community college, choose a state college that is more affordable. If you choose your community college courses carefully, every class will transfer to the four-year institution.

"Now, pay as you go. Work at least part-time to pay for your college expenses as you incur them. Surveys show that students spend less than 30 hours per week on academic work. You spend more time than that on recreation. If you'll do just two things, you'll have plenty of time to work to pay for your education: one, cut the TV time; and, two, stay out of the bars."

That exchange brought Moseley's program to a close, and he signed off for the day. Within minutes Moseley and station manager Zack Forrester came into the conference room.

"What have you learned?" Moseley asked.

"Barry began. "We have listened to recordings of all of Mike's programs over the past several months. Based on the callers' first names and cities of residence, we know that all four murder victims have called in to your program, and all expressed conservative views. In effect, all appear to be a part of a 1-800 murder scheme. Their calls appear to have put them on a kill list. Also, we have found they all lived alone, which means the murderer very likely chose victims carefully to avoid skirmishes with family members.

"The murderer had to have a way of learning the victims' phone numbers, from which full names and addresses can be determined. We believe the information had to come from someone within the WBEO organization.

"Now, what is the motive? At this point we can only speculate, but someone could be objecting to Mike's conservative political positions. Or there could be some other motive that continues to elude us. Right now we can't assume anything. We're in the process of checking to see who might have access to callers' phone numbers.

"Just in case someone on your staff disagrees with Mike's political leanings enough that they are willing to enable murder, we are checking voter registrations and have begun to run background checks on every employee. About 40% of your employees are registered Democrats, and five have been involved in left-wing protests of some sort. All five have joined groups that picketed several visiting conservative politicians and have marched to support liberal causes. They have also financially supported several liberal politicians. We have just begun this phase of our investigation. We will be learning much more."

"It sounds like Herb Bentley might be behind this," Forrester said. "He has greater access to caller information than anyone else. He's got to be at the top of your suspect list."

"Certainly he's on our list," Barry answered. "Right now nobody is excluded. Herb worked at the station every day the murders were committed, so we know Herb didn't pull the trigger. Of course, he could be providing information to a friend or accomplice who does the dirty work or to someone who arranges for the dirty work.

"Working to Herb's advantage is his personal profile.

He's 52 years old, has three grown kids, a solid marriage, stable employment, a dependable work schedule, and he lives within his income. Although there are exceptions, research shows that most crime in this country would be eliminated if every male were age 30, married, and have a job—not necessarily a good job, just a job. Herb passes all the profile tests with flying colors.

"It's true that Herb is a liberal and supports liberal causes. He came from a long family history of union membership and registered Democrats. However, to this point we can't find the intensity of purpose or the inherent anger that we would expect in a murderer."

"I have trouble believing Herb is behind this," Moseley said. "Why would he want to do something that would cause damage to my program? If my program goes off the air, he could lose his job."

"Your point is well taken," Barry answered. "I often have that same question. Still we find that most employees don't think through their actions. For instance, employees of retail stores are often rude or unhelpful to customers, not recognizing that their actions could result in reduced sales and reduced levels of employment. Airline pilots often call in sick or engage in work slow-downs during contract disputes, even though their activities often lead to the airline's failure and job losses for every employee. Most employees fail to see the big economic picture. Herb gives us the impression he understands this, but time will tell.

"Before we concentrate too much on Herb, let's not forget the five employees who have far-left leanings and could be gathering call information, possibly from some informal log that someone in the studio may be keeping.

We shouldn't be making too many assumptions at this point. Herb may be as innocent as you are. We intend to do more extensive background checks of all five left-leaners.

"Another interesting point," Barry continued, "is the four murders we know of now occurred in cities with direct flights from Columbus. We believe the murderer wanted to get in and out of town easily without the hassle of plane changes. Finally, there's another dimension of our investigation Ashley has been working on."

Ashley recounted the auto accident near Nelsonville and the word *Tomorrow* and the letters *Nu* that had been inked on the car's trunk liner.

"We are in the process of doing background checks on Stephen Bower's friends and associates, just as we are doing for your station's employees. We have no sound evidence that Bower's murder is associated with your program, but we feel we can't ignore it. Certainly there are coincidences in criminal investigations, but this is too much of a coincidence. In many cases, it's the seemingly unrelated event that brings about the solution to a crime. One interesting thing is that the security cameras at Bower's office had been deactivated the night of his murder. This could mean that someone close to Bower, such as a work associate, might have had something to do with his murder."

"What's your next move?" Moseley asked.

"We have dozens of leads yet to investigate," Barry answered, "and we'll continue on that track."

"There's something else that bothers us," Ashley interjected, "and we'd be remiss if we didn't mention it. If someone is objecting to your conservative positions so strongly they're willing to commit murder, we are somewhat concerned about your safety. Have you had any threats on your life?"

"In this business, threats on my life are a part of the work week, probably at least a dozen a week. Most are simply crank calls. But several measures are in place just in case somebody is serious.

"First, my last name isn't Moseley. That's my mother's maiden name. My real name is Eichenberger. That's too hard to pronounce and too hard to remember. Moseley is a better radio name. Also, it gives me a bit more anonymity. Of course, our close friends and neighbors know my real name, so anyone can learn my real name and where I live if they really try. But the name provides some degree of protection.

"Also, we live in a gated community, and our home is equipped with the most sophisticated security system in existence—internal and external alarms, motion detectors, video surveillance, the works. And I employ a fulltime security man who escorts my wife and kids every place they go. He did two tours in Iraq and Afghanistan with the Rangers and knows how to handle a pistol and engage in hand-to-hand combat.

"My wife and I have both had security training. No display of expensive jewelry; flat rubber soles for running. She carries her high heels in a bag. We both carry pepper spray devices and we know how to use them. It must be pointed at the guy's face. No general stuff.

"We once kept our keys out so we didn't have to fumble to open our car doors. Now with keyless cars, we never approach our cars without pepper spray in our hands. Also we avoid underground garages, we don't park next to cars where somebody can hide and ambush us, and we try to park near surveillance cameras. We never get out of the car in an insecure area.

"If anybody tries to give us a bad time, we're pretty well equipped to handle it."

"That's somewhat reassuring," Ashley said, "but if someone is willing to murder listeners, they might be willing to go to great lengths to get you off the air permanently."

"One more thing," Moseley added. "Both my wife and I are armed. We have concealed carry permits, and we're trained to use our hand guns. If somebody tries to get tough, he will wish he hadn't."

8.

For the past decade Howard Nutley has been the investment advisor to the rich and famous. He has built a high-profile reputation of consistently being able to double a person's investment quickly, often in less than 12 months, while portraying himself as a conservative investor. His 305 clients have securities portfolios with a reported aggregate market value of more than $5 billion. His reported investment returns are unequaled anywhere else in the investment world.

He has a waiting line of potential new big-name clients who want to share in his investment success. They have heard of his ability to achieve outstanding investment returns and are impressed with his lavish lifestyle—Lamborghinis, yachts, prestigious clubs, an elegant estate home, as well as his well-publicized philanthropic work.

Everything about Nutley shouts success--$6,000 Brioni suits, $2,000 Berluti shoes, and $1,000 Eton shirts. His closet must be bigger than most houses, for his clients say they seldom see him wearing the same suit or tie twice.

He walks with an air of superiority—body straight and stretched to his full height, chin in the air, a quick deliberate step. He is a man on a mission. His pride is apparent, although some see him as being a bit snooty.

Nobody questions his exceptional success. Clients and potential clients want to be able to emulate his lifestyle. "Please take me on as a client," many plead, "and I'll give you $5 million, $10 million, or even more to invest."

Reports to clients are made periodically, usually only when requested. Securities with unusually big gains are shown to have been purchased months back, substantiating huge paper profits, when in fact such investments have not been made. Clients are in awe of his ability to select consistently big gainers. When a client asks to cash out a part of or his entire investment portfolio, the cash is usually obtained from new investors. His system would make Bernie Madoff proud.

The scheme has worked successfully for the past five years. No one has questioned Nutley's ethics or integrity. His reputation as a successful community leader has given him complete credibility. He is a hometown hero.

But now things are beginning to unravel. Regulators are becoming suspicious. Inquiries are being made about possible securities fraud, investment advisor fraud, wire fraud, false statements, and misuse of customer funds.

The situation has been uncovered after regulators started to verify customer assets electronically rather than relying on paper. Regulators have alleged his bank account balance has been overstated by $5 million. He claims that accounts exist in other banks, but regulators have not been able to confirm that those accounts actually exist.

Regulators have estimated a $215 million shortfall in customer assets. Frankly, Nutley doesn't know how great the shortfall might be. He knows it is a lot, but he doesn't know how much. His Ponzi scheme has not only shielded the truth from investors and regulators but from himself as well. In the meantime, his aggressive debate with regulators, all by mail and phone, could likely drag out their investigation for a number of months, maybe even for years. As of now, no regulator has shown up in person.

Many potential new investors are in the wings to shield his scheme for a couple of years at minimum. Substantial new investments have a way of deceiving regulators, certainly for the short term, and maybe for a longer period. Nutley has enough experience with government agencies to know they are always slow, always inefficient, and usually incompetent. Thousands of investors have lost billions in savings—often their entire net worth—while federal regulators had no clue of what was going on, even when whistle blowers had provided explicit information of investment frauds. Regulator incompetence worked to Nutley's advantage.

Also working to Nutley's advantage is that most investors assume there is strict government oversight. Licensed broker-dealers who buy and sell stocks or commodities face examinations of the accounts they manage on a regular basis. But financial planners, investment advisers, retirement coaches, and others with various titles may face examination only once in a decade. The SEC reports that nearly 40% of investment advisers have never been examined or audited, not even once.

The SEC says that even with increased funding, it will be able to examine only one in ten investment advisers annually. That's another plus for Nutley. Needless to say, the federal regulators are not Nutley's primary concern.

At the outset, Nutley's plan was intended to be short term, just to make a good first impression with investors. As soon as his reputation as a very effective investment advisor had been established, and an adequate customer base had been assembled, he would cover his tracks and become a legitimate investment consultant. What could go wrong?

His plan was so easy to implement. Investors were so easy to deceive. Customers flocked to his door. They couldn't bypass investment opportunities that sounded too good to be true. It was as if they enjoyed being swindled. Soon Nutley was beyond the point of no return.

If the bubble pops now, he knew his sentence would be lengthy, maybe 25 years, maybe life. If he is able to postpone his company's demise for a few more years, his sentence might be longer. But that doesn't really matter. Life is life.

Even if he doesn't get a life sentence, he probably will not be eligible for parole. Also he will be fined and will be required to make restitution. But restitution doesn't matter, for he will never be able to pay back such substantial sums—unless he can find a way to increase his income dramatically.

He thought about it day and night. He couldn't sleep. After thorough consideration over many weeks, he decided to delay the near-certain outcome as long as possible.

He started at the top of his list of potential investors, calling first the ones he believed to be most wealthy and who have a built-in greed quality—people who are most likely to buy in to his "get richer quicker" scheme. His decision was a difficult one. He had known some of these people since high school. He attended college with some of them. He socialized with several. He liked them. He didn't want to hurt them, but he justified his actions by blaming them for being so greedy.

"I've decided to permit 30 new investors to come aboard," Nutley offered. "I intend to continue to invest funds as I have in the past, nearly assuring above-average returns. Only a few rules will be different. First, I will require a minimum investment of $10 million. And, second, new investors will not be permitted to withdraw a part or all of their investments for a period of two years. This helps me amortize my expenses over a longer period."

Every potential investor hesitated. $10 million? Tie up my funds for two years minimum?

"If you can't come up with the money" Nutley responded

casually, "that's OK. I have a waiting line of customers who can't wait to be a part of our program. If you want to step aside, someone else will gladly take your place. No pressure."

But there was pressure. No one wanted to admit they might have trouble coming up with $10 million. And no one wanted to give the impression they were unwilling to tie up those funds for two years. Their concerns about tying up huge amounts of money for two years were outweighed by their desire to share in the outlandish profits other investors had reportedly earned. New investors were given 90 days to come up with the money.

Nutley soon had 30 new investors committed, providing $300 million of new money to tide him over for a while. His only downside was that he had to wait 90 days to get his hands on it.

This infusion of new money would give him short term relief. Still he needed more money quickly—money he would not have to pay back—to ward off the fiscal cliff ahead. He must rely to a greater degree on income from his "second job."

Over the past several weeks his supplemental income had been helpful, but he knows the income from his "second job" will not begin to cover what may be a $200 million deficiency in his investment business. Or maybe it's a $500 million deficiency. He has no idea.

He has made his decision. Payment for his "second job" will have to increase. Substantially. He has no choice but to apply leverage that will increase his outside income several times over. This will give him the money he needs to pay off some investors, perpetuate his lifestyle for several more years, while continuing to advance a political ideology he believes in strongly.

9.

Ashley spent three full days interviewing investment advisors and support personnel at Stephen Bower's company. Following the interviews, she did background checks, covering everything from credit ratings, bank balances, club memberships, outstanding debts, to living standards.

Nothing unusual emerged. It was a conservative bunch. Every single one was a registered Republican. Although they were relatively successful, no one lived beyond his or her means. No one belonged to any radical organizations. As a group, she had never run into a more clean-cut staff that displayed a quality of total integrity. Ashley was impressed.

Ashley checked her list of associates. She had interviewed every person associated with the firm—except one: Howard Nutley. He was always out of the office. That didn't send up a red flag, because Nutley was known as being very successful, managing money for the community's most wealthy. He makes a lot of money and works very hard for it. Obviously he has a heavy schedule.

Ashley called for an appointment. When she arrived, Nutley was nowhere to be found. "Something came up at the last minute."

The same occurred after the second appointment. And the third. "A client called and needed to talk right away."

Ashley finally recognized this was not just a coincidence. Howard Nutley doesn't want to talk to Ashley and is going to great lengths to avoid her. She decided to get her information about Nutley elsewhere.

First, Nutley's associates were more agreeable to talking

about Nutley than she had imagined. They talked about his wealth; his flashy clothes; his fancy car; his elaborate home. He's a man who has the world by the tail.

"Does Mr. Nutley get along well with his associates?" Ashley asked several of his associates

"Well, he doesn't associate very much with the rest of us."

This attitude prevailed. Everyone was willing to talk about Nutley's conspicuous trappings of wealth, but they didn't want to talk about him as a person or as a businessman. Is this simply a sign of envy? Or is something else bothering them?

"The people I've talked to give me the impression this is one of the most ethical firms I've ever run into. Do you consider Mr. Nutley an ethical financial advisor?"

Ashley didn't expect to get a "no" answer from anyone. Most business associates won't call out unethical behavior of people they work with every day. Their eyes and facial expressions told a different story. These folks consistently did not hold Nutley in high esteem.

"What about Stephen Bower. Did he have a good relationship with Mr. Nutley?"

"He talked to Howard more than anyone else," Stephen's administrative assistant said. "But I suppose that would be natural. Their offices adjoined."

"Do you know if they ever had an argument or disagreement of some type?"

The administrative assistant had something to say. Her eyes said so. But she hesitated, not wanting to get into trouble.

"I understand your reluctance to comment," Ashley continued. "I can assure you that any comment you make will be held in strict confidence. You have my word."

"Yes, I know Stephen was not happy with some of the

things Howard was doing. I can't be specific. Stephen never shared any specifics with me. But he did question some of Howard's activities."

"Like what?"

"I don't know. Really. He told Howard that his activities would negatively affect everyone in the company and that he needed to clean up his act. That's all I know."

"Were there any threats? Or shouting matches?"

"No threats, as far as I know. Stephen was always very cool and calm. He never raised his voice. But one day Howard shouted at him to mind his own business. Everybody in the office could hear him. But, for the most part, everybody just thought that Howard was being Howard."

Ashley checked with the building manager. "Who has access to the room housing the security cameras?" she asked.

"Let's see. Not very many. Myself, of course, our maintenance guy, and Howard Nutley."

"Why Howard?" Ashley asked. "Do the other financial consultants have keys too?"

"No, just Howard. He was one of the early members of the firm. Let me think. I think there were just five of us at the time, and everybody had keys. Howard and I are the only two remaining from the original crew."

"Mr. Nutley seems to be quite a successful person. He's very well known in town. And yet I've never met him. I don't even know what he looks like. Do you have a picture of Mr. Nutley? Everybody talks about his snazzy cars and suits. What's he look like?"

"I think we have an advertising brochure that has his picture in it. Let me see. Yes, here's one. He's the guy in the second picture."

"Is this a current photo?"

"Yes, less than two years old."

"Incidentally, about how tall is Mr. Nutley?"

"He's a little guy, just 5-5. I tease him about it all the time. I ask him how it feels to play center for the Celtics, or if he knows what he wants to do when he grows up. I can tell it bugs him, but he has never lashed back at me. I can tell when he thinks I've gone over the line. Then I back off for a while."

Ashley was so surprised she sat down again. A little guy with a big house, a big car, and even bigger living. Howard Nutley is the man who was trailing her in Pittsburgh during her investigation of the Edgar Wheeler murder.

10.

"This can't go on. I've been waiting for more than two months. And nothing. I want to cash out—now—and I don't want any more excuses."

Thomas Brody, a Howard Nutley client, was speaking. Brody, 61, an owner of a precision metal manufacturer, was unloading on Nutley. "I invested $2.4 million with you two years ago. You have said it's now worth $5.1 million. I want my $5 million. I've signed a contract to buy another company, and the bank is requiring that I contribute $5 million of my own money. If I don't have the money this week, the deal is off. What's taking so long?"

"The reason I can't give you your cash now is that sometimes it takes several weeks to convert our investments into cash. We don't make the kind of investments the average Joe makes. If we did that, you wouldn't need us. You would have to accept mediocre returns. We invest in hedge funds, derivatives, and other specialized investments available only to investment pros. This is the reason we are able to produce unusually high returns."

"I understand hedge funds," Brody went on. "I understand derivatives. I understand sophisticated investments. And it doesn't take months to turn these investments into cash."

"Our investments are different. No other investment firm has produced the kinds of profits we've delivered. Tom, I'm sorry you are unhappy. We've been doing business together for a long time. I consider you my friend, and I would hate to see that friendship damaged. Is there anything I can do to restore our excellent relationship?"

"Yes, give me my money. I've been patient for more than two months. My patience has worn thin. You have had plenty of time to respond."

"I'll review your account and see what I can do."

"Howard, I'm speaking for myself, not other investors. But I can tell you I'm not alone. A dozen of us, all significant investors with you, have been meeting over the past three or four weeks. Each of us knows three or four others who are likewise expressing their concerns. It's not a pretty picture. This could blow up big time.

"Rumors are flying all over town. Many think you are running a Ponzi scheme. Frankly, I don't want to believe it. But you're not doing anything to change my mind.

"Howard, not a single investor has seen an audit of your accounts. An audit, by a Big Four accounting firm, is the only thing that will quell the vicious rumors that are becoming widely known. Again, a Big Four audit is essential. Audit reports prepared by little Mom and Pop firms too often have significant deficiencies. We want a Big Four report in two weeks."

"I can't get a Big Four auditor in here in two weeks. You are being unfair and overly demanding."

"We'll have to see which one of us is being unfair," Brody answered.

"I'll try, but I can't assure you we can pull it off."

"Unless we see a certified audit—an audit that gives us solid proof that our investments are safe—we have no choice but to order a thorough SEC audit. My company is publicly owned, and I'm a major investor in it. We make regular reports to the SEC, so we have SEC contacts we can use in making sure you are running a legitimate investment business."

""I'm disappointed you would even question whether my investment business is legitimate."

"Don't take my request casually. We are not making a casual demand. We mean business. If we don't see appropriate action soon, we have no choice but to require SEC attention.

"Please understand. Your reputation, your standard of living, your very livelihood are at stake here. Irregularities in investment accounts you manage will result in severe penalties, possibly a long prison sentence. We're in the last two minutes of the fourth quarter. The clock is about to run out. And I'm still not sure you understand the severity of the situation."

Nutley turned toward the window and could see his reflection in the plate glass. He liked to see himself there—his $6,000 suit; his $500 tie. His reflection looked bigger than life, just what Nutley enjoyed. For a few seconds he admired his image, nearly forgetting the nature of Brody's demands.

"Can we expect action now?" Brody said. "Or will it be up to us to implement appropriate measures? I can tell you with certainty that a number of your investors are willing and anxious to take more severe steps than those I have suggested. It will be to your advantage to avoid the dire actions some investors want to take."

Nutley looked unwavering and confident. This is just a game—a game he'd always won. He felt he would win this one too. "I'll see what I can do," he said.

Brody has been a successful businessman for a long time. He has thousands of employees. He is a good judge of human nature. He feels strongly that Nutley does not intend to order a Big Four audit. He is convinced Nutley is operating a Ponzi scheme.

11.

Howard Nutley initiated the call. "It's me. A couple of blocks off High Street in the Short North there's a flea bag hotel called Ace Motel."

"Yes. I know where it is."

"Meet me at 8 o'clock. Room 7."

"Regarding what?"

"I'll tell you when you get there. There's a restaurant parking lot a couple of blocks away. Park there and walk to the motel. Be there."

"You know you're not supposed to call me. And we're never ever supposed to meet in public. What's so urgent we have to meet? This had better be good."

"Settle down," Nutley answered. "Hundreds of strangers from the convention center are buzzing around everywhere. Nobody will notice two more people. We're more anonymous here than anyplace in town."

The Short North had been a depressed area just north of the downtown. When the convention center was built on the site of the old Union Station, renovation and new building began, with dozens of trendy restaurants and shops that attract both conventioneers and locals.

The developers' wrecking ball hadn't yet found the Ace Motel. The building was probably more than 50 years old and hadn't had more than one paint job since it was built. Shingles were missing from the composition roof. Purple carpet, purple bedspread, both needed cleaning badly. No, they needed to be replaced. The room was reminiscent of the TV commercial in which the occupant is wearing a space suit and gas mask. The ill-fitting door let light into the room. This place couldn't begin to qualify for a tax credit for energy efficiency. On a scale of one to ten, this motel rated a point five.

"This had better be important. What's this meeting all about?"

"So far our plan has gone smoothly. But the one in St. Louis may be a problem. Not sure about fingerprints and DNA. If the police do a thorough investigation, my neck could be on the chopping block. A policeman investigating the stolen car became suspicious. Asked my name and I stumbled. I could tell he thought it was odd I couldn't remember my name. At that time the murder had not been reported, but when it is, he is likely to add two and two.

"Now this PI is snooping around. What's her name? Alexander, Ashley Alexander. A good looking gal but tough. I followed her to Pittsburgh, and she knows what she's doing. Now she's snooping around my office. Spending a lot of time there. Looking under all the rocks. Don't know what she'll find, but it's getting uncomfortable. So far I've avoided her, but I know it's just a matter of time."

"So? What do you think this is, tick-tac-toe? Of course, things will get uncomfortable once in a while. You knew that before this started."

"With the pressures that are building," Nutley said, "I've decided I can't work for the amount you're paying. It's just not worth it. If I'm going to continue, I have to have a lot more."

"You've got to be kidding. You're being paid more than you're worth. Moreover, if we stay on course, you're benefiting just as much as I am. Both of us want the same thing. You should be working for nothing."

"I have decided the contribution I'm making is worth substantially more. Why should I be risking my career and my life?"

"How much do you want?"

"For starters, I must have a one-time payment of $25 million. In cash."

"$25 million. You must be nuts! I don't have that kind of money."

"Well, maybe you'd better find a way to get it."

"If that's the way you want it, I'm willing to discontinue our relationship. You're not the only fish in the sea. I can find someone better than you to carry out the plan."

"Not so fast. The FBI will be happy to learn of your involvement. You don't have any choice in the matter."

"If I'm charged for being an accomplice to murder, you're going to go down with me. If you blow the whistle on me, you'll be blowing it on yourself."

"That doesn't really matter anymore. My investment business is falling apart. The feds have been sending nasty letters and threatening phone calls. Now some of my clients are on the war path, want a Big Four audit, and are threatening to call in the SEC. Once the dust settles, I'll probably go to prison. Maybe for life. Speeding up the process a bit really doesn't make that much difference. As I said, you don't have a choice. It's $25 million, period. You might say it's sort of a signing bonus. After the signing bonus, the payment for each assignment will double"

"There's no way. I haven't got the money, can't get the money, and it's not worth the money. Maybe it's time to call it quits. Stop it in its tracks. It's the end of the show."

"That's not the way it's going to work. It's $25 million whether we stop or go. I have nothing to lose. You have everything to lose."

"That's blackmail!"

"Exactly. And I intend to collect it. Maybe you'd better seriously consider your options."

Both men sat in silence for a few minutes. Nutley spoke first. "Is the meeting over?"

Again, there was silence for a full two minutes. "I'll have to think about this." He opened the door and walked slowly to his car.

12.

Wearing worn and faded jeans, shirt, and shoes he wears when he washes the car or works around the house, Barry tried to melt in with a sizable crowd that had begun to assemble. Still Barry felt overdressed. Other than one person in the room, most in attendance made Occupy Wall Streeters look like conservative investment bankers. The organization is called GAFF, an acronym that stands for Government Affording a Fair Future.

Soon more than a hundred people had gathered, and what a motley crew it was! Only one person was dressed business casual—casual but sharp. Barry recognized him right away from a picture Ashley had given him. It was Howard Nutley. Ashley's investigation had found that Nutley was actively involved with this far-left activist group and several other liberal political movements. Barry knew who Nutley was, but Nutley didn't know Barry. Nutley's expensive clothing and a watch valued greater than the net worth of most attendees made him stand out. Barry thought it was interesting that many in the group despised the rich, but not the rich that embraced their liberal views.

Most members of the crowd were the homeless, welfare recipients, radical students, modern day hippies, and other misfits of society. The group stormed the refreshment tables when they entered. They appeared to be more interested in the food than in whatever topics might be discussed.

Nutley was in charge and called the meeting to order. Minutes after the meeting began, a familiar face came into the room—Herb Bentley, Moseley's call screener. Bentley immediately recognized Barry, appeared embarrassed, wanted a way out, but didn't know how to get out without making his presence even more obvious. Bentley settled into the back row, looked very uncomfortable, glanced at Barry periodically, but remained quiet throughout the meeting.

The first order of business was a demonstration in connection with the visit the following week by Paul Mayfair, a conservative candidate for the U.S. Senate.

"We want at least a thousand people there," Nutley shouted. "Tell all your friends. We'll have signs for you, a box lunch, and $30 for cab fare," and then he went on to say that buses will pick up participants at four pick-up points. The group applauded lightly. No one questioned Mayfair's political philosophy or what issues he supported that the group might be opposed to, but certainly a box lunch and $30 got their attention.

Two weeks later there would be another visit by a conservative politician, and similarly GAFF would provide signs, box lunches, $30 cab fare, and buses to the meeting site.

The room was overcrowded; the air conditioner was running full blast but couldn't keep up with the demands of a sweaty audience. And Nutley's sweat glands were likewise working overtime as he continued to wipe his face with tissues.

Nutley opened the meeting to questions. One called for extended unemployment benefits. "Three years are not enough. We should be able to get unemployment benefits for at least five years," he said, and the group applauded modestly.

"Free child care," another said. "We need to be able to go to the store, or go to meetings, or just get away from the kids for a while. It's unfair to saddle us with the kids while the rich people run around and do anything they want to do whenever they want to do it." Again there was light applause.

When the group applauded, Barry clapped along, not wanting anyone to question his presence. But Bentley remained quiet, the only one in the room who did not show his support of the issues being discussed.

Not many topics were overlooked—more generous eligibility for food stamps, and greater freedom to use food stamps for purchases other than food. The crowd applauded with a bit more enthusiasm.

Free university tuition, and the crowd applauded, even though most probably couldn't spell university.

"Tax the rich," one person yelled. "How rich?" another asked. "Family income over $30,000," the first man responded.

Free health care, birth control, abortion on demand, income equality, family planning, no voter suppression, expanded welfare benefits, energy assistance, additional public housing, animal rights, and even world peace were called for, all with modest applause. No one issue was a hot button. The group gave only light obligatory response to any topic mentioned.

About the only thing missing was a call for more jobs. With the benefits these folks were demanding, who needed to work?

"We've got a good crowd here today," Nutley said as he prepared to close the meeting, "but we want more next month. We need to show the world that we're a strong voice; we need to show the politicians they must pay attention to us or we'll vote them out of office. We are a force to be reckoned with, and we won't stop until our numbers overshadow the Tea Party."

A man near Barry turned to his neighbor and said, "I don't

like tea. I like beer and black coffee."

Nutley closed the meeting by announcing the date and time of the next meeting. "We're not going to have just punch and cookies. We're going to have a full spaghetti and meat ball dinner. All you can eat, with garlic bread, pie and ice cream. Bring all your friends, and let's make this the biggest meeting in our history."

For the first time all evening, there was wild, enthusiastic applause. Spaghetti and meat balls. That's something everyone believed in.

As the meeting ended, clusters of people gathered around the room to chat, and many gathered to claim what remained at the refreshment table. The crowd paid no mind to Barry as he moved to the front of the room and, as unobtrusively as possible, placed Nutley's disposed tissues in a small plastic bag. Barry had a feeling that a sample of Nutley's DNA might come in handy.

As Barry made his way across the parking lot, he stopped to survey the crowd. Bentley and Nutley were talking near the building's entryway. Bentley was pointing toward Barry. Now Nutley knew that the Barry/Ashley team is monitoring Nutley's activities.

13.

Howard Nutley remained in his office late into the evening reflecting on the problems surrounding his investment business and trying to evaluate possible courses of action.

His demand for a $25 million payment had gone unanswered. Obviously he needed to become more persuasive, but not so persuasive that he kills the goose that lays the golden egg. So murder is out, at least for now. Maybe just a good beating will get the desired results.

Those two PIs are troublesome. Should he take them out? Or would this bring about even greater scrutiny from law enforcement agencies? Or is there a half-way approach—something that will scare their socks off and cause them to withdraw from their investigation?

Now some of his clients are on the war path. Tom Brody had always been reasonable and patient, but his patience is now wearing thin. Some of the other clients Brody has been talking to may not be so reasonable and patient, and a few of them may take action against Nutley that may not be so pleasant.

The rumor mill is becoming more active. More and more ripples about his investment practices were emerging throughout the community. He had given his 30 new clients 90 days to come up with $300 million of new money. All had been more than eager to participate. But as rumors spread, the likelihood is increasing that one or more will withdraw. And as the word spreads that investors' money may be in jeopardy, more and more of his existing clients will be requesting the withdrawal of their funds.

Topping all this off are regulatory concerns. Brody has promised an SEC audit. Then today two additional regulatory agencies, the Commodity Futures Trading Commission and the industry's self-regulatory body, the National Futures Association, have begun to hassle Nutley. Both have filed separate enforcement actions against Nutley, alleging falsified bank statements to cover shortfalls in client funds. Thanks to career bureaucrats and regulatory incompetence, Nutley was more concerned about the industry association than the government agency. Although it will require time to comply with the agencies' requests, Nutley didn't consider either a big deal. He hoped to have $300 million of additional funds from new investors. With that money, he would be able to paper over any obvious shortfalls for the short term. If the $300 million payment does not materialize, the problem will be more severe.

He isn't all that concerned about fixing the problems for the very long term. Deep down he knows his entire business operation will unravel sooner or later. Right now his long term is a week at a time, although he remains optimistic he can keep his problems under cover for several years. He isn't sure what he will do, but he has always worked something out, often at the last minute, so he is convinced he can do it again.

Nutley's Ponzi scheme has worked well for five years. With new investors coming aboard, he is sure he can keep it going for another five years. Maybe ten years. Maybe longer. Regulatory intrusion is the least of his worries. So far the regulators had only nibbled around the edges and have never looked into the more serious core problems.

His view of regulators fits well with his political philosophy overall. The bigger the government, the more unmanageable government becomes. The more unmanageable government becomes, the more incompetent government bureaucracy becomes. The more incompetent government bureaucracy becomes, the less likely his deceitful business operations will become known. Howard Nutley loves big, bureaucratic government. Big government fits him to a tee.

He placed his problems in priority order—(1) apply leverage to collect the $25 million he has demanded. This is money that's his—immediately. It doesn't have to be paid back. It's all under the table. He doesn't have to give part of it to IRS. It's like money from the Tooth Fairy. There is no record of it anyplace. And it's in his pocket to spend whenever he wishes and for whatever he wishes.

(2) Get the two PIs off his back. They are digging much deeper than he had initially believed they would. They are uncovering too much. They must be dealt with—somehow.

(3) Keep the 30 new investors and their $300 million of new money in the pipeline. He must encourage them to ignore any ugly rumors they may hear. Nutley considers himself an expert in BS. He has built his investment business by schmoozing and talking a good game. He must use these skills to keep the new investors on course.

(4) Now, what should he do about unrest among current investors? Schmoozing and over-promising aren't working as well with this group. They want investment results, certainly, but they also want access to their money on demand. This group will be harder to persuade.

(5) Keep the financial regulators at bay. This is the least of his concerns. He thanked God for bureaucratic incompetence.

He decided to devote his primary attention to number one, and throw a good scare at the PIs as a close number two. The other issues will wait—they *must* wait.

It was after midnight when Nutley left the office, walked to his new black Lamborghini and drove to his palatial home on the outskirts of Dublin, a northwest Columbus suburb. He parked in the covered drive in front of his home, opened the car door, slid out from behind the wheel, started toward his front door when a gunshot whizzed overhead. Nutley hit the ground and crawled to the opposite side of the car. Another shot rang out.

He remained still for a few minutes, apparently out of sight of the shooter. The front door was locked, and he knew he couldn't take the time to get to the door, unlock it, and get inside. He would be an easy target for the shooter. His best option would be to run around the side of the house and enter through a back door, although he considered the possibility another shooter could be stationed behind the house. He had to take the chance.

Ready, set, run! As he turned the corner at the side of the house, another shot rang out. Upon entering the house, he actually had to check to see if he had been hit. With the rush of adrenaline, he had read that shooting victims sometimes didn't know they had been wounded. Now Nutley understood how this could be. He saw no blood so he assumed he was OK.

He remained still, away from the windows, with the lights out. After nearly an hour, he crept upstairs, with the lights still out, and went to bed. But sleep did not come easily.

Nutley reviewed his priorities. He was certain regulators wouldn't try to kill him. He could leave his regulatory problems at the bottom of the list. He was just as certain the two PIs would not try to shoot him. This is not how they operate. He could leave the private detectives as priority number two.

The thirty new clients? While rumors were beginning to emerge, he was certain at this point they were not so disillusioned that any of them would attempt murder. His schmoozing objective would continue.

Current clients? Tom Brody is intelligent, demanding, and means business, but he is not a violent man. Some of the others he may be talking to could become violent. Several that came to mind are not as nice as Brody. He needs to pay off those who have requested the return of their investment, but they will just have to wait. There is no option until the new investors come aboard. If they come aboard.

Of all potential shooters, Nutley felt certain the shots were tied to his demand for $25 million. He is nearly 100% certain of the identity of the person who took shots at him. His priority number one moved up a few degrees in importance.

His question is: What can he do about it? How can he eliminate the potential murderer before the murderer eliminates him?

"Ashley, you might find this interesting." Win Jent, Ashley's and Barry's police friend, was on the phone.

"You've been doing some background checks on associates of Stephen Bower. You said you are especially interested in Howard Nutley.

"Nutley may have been involved in some unusual activities last night. Four of Nutley's neighbors called the Dublin police early this morning to report they heard gun shots at about 1 a.m. All believe the sound was at or near Nutley's home.

"Of course, sometimes it's hard to know where sounds originate, because sounds bounce off buildings, retaining walls, or other hard objects.

"Dublin police called on Nutley at about two o'clock this

morning. Nutley said he went to bed at about 11 p.m. and had not heard shots or any other commotion. He said his neighbors must have been mistaken."

"Was the neighborhood checked for shell casings or other evidence of a shooter in the area?" Ashley asked.

"It wasn't in their report. They may be doing a further investigation today, but that's all we have now."

"I think we'll check it out," Ashley added.

Her first stop was to see if Nutley's car was parked at his office. She didn't want to snoop around Nutley's home if he happened to be home at the time. Nutley's black Lamborghini was in his assigned spot at his office lot. She walked around the car, checking it carefully, and found a bullet hole had entered the left front window and had exited on the right side of the car.

Ashley drove to Nutley's home in Dublin. She found three bullet holes in the front of the house and pried the bullets from the wooden siding, being careful not to damage the ballistic fingerprint. They were .30-06 cartridges, used by the Army for some 50 years and still popular with sportsmen.

The angle of the bullet's entry would indicate the shots were fired from a wooded area in a park across the street, some 150 yards from Nutley's home.

Ashley walked through the park looking for places a shooter could have hidden. Footprints were everywhere—some adults, some children. It was a popular neighborhood playground. Heavy use made it impossible to identify the footprints of a gunman. She could find no shell casings or other evidence the shooter left behind. However, there were several spots that would have given a gunman a clear shot at Nutley's house, and any number of high power rifles would have been accurate at 150 yards if the shooter was a good marksman and the scope had been properly adjusted for wind conditions and gravity. Considering the space between the bullet holes, the shooter was either a poor marksman or the target was moving.

Ashley's next stop was with the manager of the building housing Nutley's office.

"Do you remember me?" Ashley began. "I was here a few days ago interviewing associates of Stephen Bower."

"Yes, I remember you well. I am impressed with the thoroughness of your investigation."

"I have another request. Could I review last night's security tape?"

The manager didn't question Ashley's request and gave her full access to the system.

"Can we be sure the time indication on the tape is accurate?" Ashley asked. "That is, if it says 12 o'clock, can we be sure it's 12 o'clock?"

"We've never checked it," the manager answered, "but as far as I know it's right."

Ashley ran the tape several times. There was no question. Nutley left the office and walked to his car at 12:39 a.m. He had not gone to bed at 11 p.m. as he claimed. Nutley knows more about last night's disturbances than he acknowledged to Dublin police.

14.

"No Tomorrow" was the rallying cry of GAFF chapters across the country, setting the stage for a countrywide demonstration of radio stations carrying Moseley's *Tomorrow* radio show. It was scheduled for the first Tuesday of the following month. Predictions were that hundreds of thousands of demonstrators would show up at the 500 or so radio stations airing Moseley's program. The demonstrators would demand greater government spending on a myriad of taxpayer-funded programs intended to help America's less fortunate and the country's middle class.

As expected, demonstrations by left-wing radical groups tend to get lots of news coverage from the nation's liberal media. "No Tomorrow" was no exception. It was the lead story of all the national TV network newscasts and in newspapers in every major city.

Moseley decided to fight back. Moseley announced his own FAA day for that same Tuesday.

"FAA isn't another federal agency. It means Flags Across America," Moseley told his about 15 million listeners. "I'm asking every home in America to fly an American flag.

"Frankly, demonstrations are unproductive and silly. Most demonstrators don't even know why they are demonstrating. Most demonstrations are recreation for participants. It's a walk in the park. So on FAA day our demonstration will be different. The American flag is a symbol of your support of our great country and the principles our flag represents. It's a symbol of the freedoms we enjoy in America, and it's a statement that we will not let those freedoms be destroyed by liberal politicians and activists. It's a symbol of the great opportunities America offers each and every one of us. And it's a symbol of the economic opportunities available to anyone who wants to work to achieve them.

"If you don't have a flag, this network is making it possible for you to buy a flag conveniently and economically. All Walmart and Target stores, as well as other major retail outlets throughout the country, will be making three by five American flags available for the subsidized cost of only $2.95.

"Not only will you be showing your support of America by flying your flag, you will be supporting our fragile economy, for these flags are all made in America.

"Flying a flag is the kind of demonstration that makes sense. It's the kind of demonstration our forefathers would be proud of. Just think about it—no community disturbances, no taxpayer cost for crowd or traffic control, no danger to our citizens—just a strong show of support for the greatest country in the world.

"And we can fly our flags and be a part of this worthwhile and patriotic demonstration without taking a day off from work. Work—now that's a term many demonstrators are not familiar with."

When FAA day (or No Tomorrow day) arrived, most major cities were seas of red, white and blue. Moseley was overwhelmed with the widespread support being shown across the country.

At about noon a crowd began to gather at the WBEO parking lot in preparation for the 2 p.m. demonstration. They gathered under a tree at the edge of the parking lot where they ate their box lunches. Then someone distributed envelopes containing their $30 cab fares.

Moseley took his microphone and digital recorder into

the parking lot. No one seemed to know Moseley was the talk show host whose program was being picketed. Moseley moved from person to person, asking questions and recording answers.

"Are you happy with the programs of our current President, Bill Loney?" Most answered "yes" or "I guess so."

"Do you believe our vice president, Bonnie Ann Clyde, is qualified to take over as President if President Loney should die unexpectedly?" Everyone answered in the affirmative. Most said they had heard of the good work being performed by Vice President Clyde and have confidence in her ability to lead the nation.

"What policies of President Loney do you especially like or dislike?" Most answered "I don't know," although several said "I need more money."

"Do you believe our Secretary of State, Chris Cross, is doing a good job of maintaining relationships with foreign countries?" This question was a little harder. No one seemed to understand the question or even attempted an answer.

"President Loney is proposing that a new Cadillac be provided to every citizen. Do you think that's a good idea?" This drew the most enthusiastic responses: "Yeow!"

"What do you hope to accomplish with your demonstration today?" Moseley continued. Answers were hard to draw out, although one said, "I like the car idea."

"The problem President Loney is having is getting the money to pay for the new Cadillacs. Where do you think he should get the money?" One demonstrator answered, "Why does he have to get the money? It's Loney money." Several said "the rich," and most neighboring demonstrators agreed.

"What percentage of their income should the rich pay in taxes?" Moseley asked of several demonstrators. No one quite understood the question.

"Should the rich pay 10%, 20%, 50% of their income to the government?" Moseley continued. Again, no one could relate to the term percentage.

"Let me try again. Should the rich pay $100 a year in taxes, $500, or $ 1,000 a year in taxes?" The first three demonstrators he asked felt that $1,000 a year would be about right.

Today's *Tomorrow* program primarily consisted of the interviews Moseley conducted in the parking lot. His message to listeners was clear: Demonstrators don't know why they are demonstrating; have no understanding of government and its structure; and have no understanding of taxes and government spending. The interviews were not a tribute to America's education system.

At the height of today's demonstrations, about 150 people had gathered in the WBEO parking lot. News reports across the country suggested that only a sprinkling of demonstrators visited other radio stations carrying the *Tomorrow* program.

The WBEO demonstration was peaceful for nearly two hours as they marched with signs reading "No Tomorrow," which sounded like they were predicting the end of the world, or the word "Tomorrow" in a circle with a slash through the circle. One sign said "End the Republican Agenda," and another read "Citizens for a Better Tomorrow." Clearly, the demonstrators were not passionate about any subject except the box lunch and the $30 cab fare.

As the demonstrators prepared to enter the buses for transportation back to their home communities, something sparked their action. The crowd broke into two groups, dashed across the parking lot, and overturned two cars—two cars not parked together. The cars were doused with gasoline and set afire.

One car was station manager Zack Forrester's Lexus 460. The other was Mike Moseley's GMC Yukon XL Denali. No other cars were damaged.

The demonstrators ran back to their buses, which left immediately. Overturning and burning the cars took only two or three minutes as police watched passively.

15.

It was nearly four o'clock, the time Barry and Ashley normally met with Mike Moseley and station manager Zack Forrester. The WBEO receptionist escorted Barry and Ashley to the station's conference room. They could hear a caller to Mike's program on the conference room speakers.

"The support of your FAA program was unbelievable," the caller said. "I've never seen so many American flags being flown—not on Independence Day, not on Flag Day, not on Veterans Day. It gave me encouragement that the majority of people feel as I do—government is too big, too expensive, too corrupt, and the American people are ready to do something about it. I just want to thank you for getting this movement going."

"And I thank you for your support and your call," Moseley replied. "I too was pleased and surprised at the support we received. I think it's clear the American people are anxious to get our government back on track, serving the people instead of government insiders."

Several calls followed, all expressing gratitude and enthusiastic support of FAA. If any calls were received, none were aired from the "No Tomorrow" movement. Probably most supporters were cowering with embarrassment because of the small turnouts and weak public acceptance of their efforts.

Moseley's interviews of demonstrators received rave reviews from the public across the country. The demonstrators appeared uninformed, uneducated, uninvolved, and unwilling to work to care for themselves or to contribute to society generally, and the general public resented the attention the demonstrators were getting from the main-stream media.

Shortly after Moseley signed off, he and Forrester entered the conference room.

"Congratulations on the tremendously successful FAA day," Ashley began. "You must be pleased with the positive public reception."

"It was more successful than we ever imagined," Moseley answered. "The main-stream media gave the GAFF group its primary attention. But several polling organizations have been at work, and the initial reports show clearly the public supports our position two to one."

"Was there any violence across the country, other than your cars being overturned and burned?" Barry asked.

"This was the only damage reported," Forrester answered. "I guess that's a small price to pay for airing programs that some listeners see as controversial. It was no big deal. The cars can be replaced."

"Where does your investigation stand?" Moseley asked.

"We've made significant progress," Barry answered, "but I'm afraid we still don't have enough evidence to prosecute."

"We're anxious to get your update," Forrester said.

"We can say with certainty," Ashley began, "that Howard Nutley has more than a passive interest in the murders that have occurred. He followed me to Pittsburgh when I did my investigation there. As a matter of fact, I approached him. I talked to him face to face. At the time I didn't know he was Howard Nutley. I found that he had rented a car using an alias of Carl Bristol. He used a fake driver's license and credit card using Bristol's name and a non-existent Columbus address. Does this prove guilt? Certainly not. This bit of evidence just contributes to a near-certain conclusion that Nutley is somehow involved with the murders.

"You may recall the murder of Stephen Bower, a young financial consultant who inked the word *Tomorrow* followed by the letters *Nu* on the trunk liner of his car before the car and Bower's body were torched," Ashley continued. "Bower and Howard Nutley were financial consultants in the same firm, working in adjacent offices. We believe Bower was attempting to write the word *Nutley* on the trunk liner to tell us Nutley is involved with the *Tomorrow* murders, but he didn't finish the job before he was brutally murdered.

"I've spent a good deal of time interviewing and doing background checks of Bower's and Nutley's associates. I do not believe Bower and Nutley had a business disagreement that resulted in Bower's murder. All members of the firm own their own business, serve their own clients, and receive commissions from the services they provide. All members of the firm pay a percentage of their income to the firm for office space, advertising, secretarial help, and other overhead costs. We find no evidence that business disputes brought about Bower's murder.

"On the other hand, we know that Bower had discussions with Nutley on his business practices. We don't know what prompted their discussions. Perhaps he overheard a conversation Nutley may have had with someone. When doing my interviews I noted the cubicle walls are very thin. They certainly aren't sound proofed. I could hear muffled voices next door. Had we remained quiet, I'm sure we could have made out discussions of neighbors.

"It appears to us Bower tried to do the right thing, although his actions likely resulted in his death. He talked to Nutley about what he overheard. We believe this may have led to Bower's murder being committed by Nutley or at his direction."

"It sounds like Nutley is our guy," Forrester interjected. "You say we still don't have enough evidence to convict?"

"We have some evidence," Barry answered, "but its circumstantial evidence that won't stand alone."

"Fingerprints were found on the side of the house of the murder victim in St. Louis as well as in the stolen car in St. Louis," Ashley continued. "The prints were smudged badly and could not be specifically traced. However, there were print similarities with Nutley's prints taken by the Securities Division of the Ohio Department of Commerce when he obtained his securities license. But again, similarities won't cut it. This bit of evidence contributes to a conclusion but it cannot stand alone.

"DNA evidence was also recovered from the stolen car. At this point there is no match in the DNA data base, but that should be remedied shortly. Barry gathered some of Nutley's DNA at the local GAFF meeting. This has been turned over to the police lab. Very soon we should know if Nutley was involved in the St. Louis murder. This, along with all the circumstantial evidence we have cited, should be the clincher we're looking for. If we get a DNA match, we think we can make a charge that will stick. The only gap will be where he got his caller information. This is still a missing piece of the puzzle."

"The evidence is pretty clear," Forrester interrupted. "You're building a strong case against Nutley."

"Yes, strong," Ashley answered, "but not strong enough, even though there's still more. Another piece of evidence contributes to the same conclusion. Airline passenger lists are not made public to respect passengers' privacy, but law enforcement agencies are allowed to access that information if they have a legitimate reason. With assistance from our law enforcement friends, we have found that Howard Nutley made trips to each of the cities where murders occurred on the dates they occurred.

"Of course, this does not prove his involvement with the murders. It could have been a mere coincidence—an unlikely coincidence, but still a coincidence. If he made an appearance in court, you can bet he would have good reasons for his presence on those dates, such as visiting a client or potential client. It would be impossible to prove his involvement in murders on the basis of passenger lists alone. Still further, this evidence would probably not be accepted by a court of law because we may have violated Nutley's right to privacy in obtaining this information.

"There's still more circumstantial evidence," Ashley continued. "Ballistics tells us that different hand guns were used in the various murders. We can't specifically identify any weapon that hasn't previously been involved in a crime and for which a ballistics print has been stored. The murder weapon must have been acquired locally, and Nutley has resources that can provide murder weapons.

"We have found that Nutley is a gun collector and is a member of the Gun Hobbyists Society of America. A number of members of GHSA are located in cities in which the murders have taken place. We've checked with the police departments of those cities and have learned that most members are just that—hobbyists or collectors. They operate lawfully and sell guns only to other collectors. Some members, however, are ethically challenged and may well provide guns to persons who have some type of criminal activity in mind."

"To me it sounds like we have a clear-cut case. That should

be all the evidence we need," Forrester interjected.

"Certainly a lot of evidence points to Nutley," Barry added, "but at this point we would be laughed out of court. There's simply no absolute evidence at this time.

"We got from detectives the names of GHSA members in the various cities who they believe are most likely to violate gun laws. We talked to several who might have provided weapons to Nutley, but our visits weren't productive. Some simply wouldn't talk to us. Others had severe cases of self-imposed Alzheimer's. They aren't going to implicate themselves in a possible crime. Their appearance in court would not advance our position.

"All this information combined can supplement that one solid piece of evidence that cannot be questioned, but right now we don't have it. Right now we have to wait for a possible DNA match from the stolen car. Then we'll have a pretty solid case."

"Nutley has a strong ideological motivation to want you off the air, Mike," Ashley said. "He has far left radical leanings and is actively involved in several radical movements. He is one of the founders of GAFF and was instrumental in picketing this station and other stations airing your program.

"We interviewed a number of the demonstration participants at the homeless shelter just off I-71 downtown. The individuals we interviewed were not defensive and did not fear retribution by sharing information with us. They saw it as their duty to carry out orders they received from others.

"Based on a picture of Nutley we showed them, they confirmed that Howard Nutley was the one who gave them orders to burn your two cars in the WBEO parking lot. They had pictures and license numbers of both cars."

"At least can't we convict for burning our cars?" Forrester asked.

"That's possible," Barry answered. "Burning your cars is one charge that might stick. He might be convicted for something as minor as malicious mischief or vandalism. He would likely get a slap on the wrist and would be back in business the next day. I doubt that this is the way you would want to deal with Mr. Nutley. Furthermore, even this charge would require good witnesses that are persuasive in court. Although they were open to us, the demonstrators will likely resort to total silence should they be brought into the uncomfortable environment of a courtroom. These folks will not be good witnesses.

"If Nutley is the murderer," Barry continued, "we still don't know how he obtained the phone numbers of the murder victims. Your call screener is certainly a suspect because of his ready access to that information and his interest in GAFF. Herb Bentley was highly embarrassed when he came into the GAFF meeting and recognized me in the audience.

"Background checks tell us 40% of your station's employees are liberals and may be resentful of Mike's conservative philosophies. We believe only five are somewhat active with liberal organizations and contribute money to them, so their names rank a little higher on the suspect list. Herb is the most likely one who could provide caller information to Nutley or someone else outside your organization, but we have no solid evidence he is involved."

"One final thing," Ashley added. "We have learned that several regulatory agencies are investigating Nutley's investment business. Apparently there is some evidence Nutley may be misusing customer funds. We don't know how serious the problem is, but we know rumors are flying throughout the investment community and several of his associates expect SEC auditors to show up any day. We're not sure how this bears on his possible involvement in murders, but there could be a relationship.

"We checked Nutley's bank records, and, boy, what a mess," Ashley went on. "One day he has a balance of more than a million dollars. The next day he's overdrawn by a half million. From our cursory review, we couldn't tell if he is comingling his personal funds with customer funds. It will take a full-blown audit to untangle it. We can only say his financial situation looks fishy.

"Somebody took a shot at Nutley's car and his home in Dublin, and we suspect someone was shooting at Nutley himself. We have a good ballistic print of the bullet, but it doesn't match any weapon in the NIBIN ballistic database. Therefore, the bullet can't lead us to the shooter until we find the weapon.

"Why would someone want to take Nutley out? It might relate to his involvement with the radical GAFF group. Or a disgruntled investor may be upset with Nutley if he believes his money has evaporated in an investment scam. Or it could relate to the murders we are investigating. The motive for the attempt on Nutley's life should become more clear as our investigation develops."

Barry and Ashley stopped talking. There was total silence for a full two minutes while Forrester and Moseley tried to absorb the information Barry and Ashley had provided.

Finally Barry broke the silence. "We hope you'll agree that we have made considerable progress. We hope you'll agree that we're getting closer to breaking this case."

"I'm pleased with the progress you've made," Moseley said. "We can't let this guy damage my program and the reputation of this station. We must do what we have to do to build a case that will hold up in court."

Moseley looked at Forrester to get concurrence, but Forrester's mind was in a cloud, apparently trying to absorb all the ramifications of the case.

"We believe we are very close to breaking open this case," Ashley said. "We are very close to having specific evidence that will, without question, identify the murderer. We're just days away. We feel quite confident about it."

16.

Substantial progress was being made with Barry's and Ashley's investigation. Things were falling into place quickly, and they were confident murder charges could be filed soon. Then a bombshell fell.

"I just know he's guilty," Ashley said emphatically. "I just know a good DNA match would have identified Nutley as the murderer. The DNA should have tied Nutley to the St. Louis murder, and circumstantial evidence would have led to his involvement in the other three murders. We had built a case that would have put Nutley away for life. Now we're back to square one. I'm at a loss as to our next step."

Ashley and Barry were discussing their investigation as they had dinner together late one evening at the Brio Tuscan Grill at Easton.

DNA tests are believed to be extremely accurate. And for the most part they are. But they are in error more often than commonly reported. They had just received a report from the police lab that Nutley's DNA test was in error. Nutley's DNA sample was degraded because the sample was too old or had been exposed to such harsh conditions it could not be read accurately. Also, the DNA sample contained a mixture of three alleles in one of the loci tested. In other words, more than one person contributed to the sample, probably the owner or previous driver of the stolen car.

"We shouldn't be so hard on ourselves," Barry said. "Things happen for a reason. Maybe this is a way of telling us our case still isn't sound. We still have some work to do.

"Even with a clean DNA reading, Nutley's attorney would have probably acknowledged that Nutley indeed stole a car in St. Louis. Then he would try to prove he had nothing to do with the murder. Only the smudged fingerprints found outside the house of the murder victim would have tied him to the murder. Because the prints were badly smudged, it would not have been a slam dunk. This new problem is simply a signal to us that we don't have enough indisputable evidence that will hold up in court."

Ashley didn't comment for several minutes. She was terribly disappointed with the DNA test, and the disappointment was affecting her normal positive frame of mind.

"Look, DNA test or no DNA test, something is missing from this picture," Barry went on. "If Nutley is as guilty as we think he is, he is getting caller information from someone—probably someone in the WBEO organization. So we know someone else is involved, at least to the degree of providing caller information. That person may be someone even more important. Maybe a Big Boss is giving orders to Nutley.

"Even if we were able to arrest Nutley now, the Big Boss, if one actually exists, may go unpunished unless Nutley implicates him. And we can't be sure of his allegiances to that person or persons. Because his investment business is coming unglued, he may be willing to take the hit and let others go unpunished."

"This means we change our emphasis?" Ashley asked. "You're saying we should prod away at all potential suspects, even remote ones, and continue to gather more substantial evidence. When we locate the Big Boss, we can come in the back door to get Nutley."

"That's right. The more information we gather, the more likely others involved will get nervous, make a mistake, shed light on the big picture, implicate the Big Boss, and we can bring Nutley along in the shuffle. Also, we may yet get a good DNA sample for Nutley."

As is so often true in the cases they are pursuing, Barry and Ashley had become so deeply engrossed in this case they had lost track of time. The restaurant was nearly empty, and the wait staff and bussers had become impatient with the dawdlers. They were ready to go home.

Barry and Ashley obliged, left the restaurant, drove to their Worthington apartment, and parked their car. They walked toward their apartment's front door, when a shot rang out—a shot from a high powered rifle. They instinctively hit the ground behind a decorative concrete spindle and rail fence. The spindles provided some protection, but if a bullet hit the gap between the spindles, they were in deep trouble.

Three shots were fire. Then all was quiet.

After about ten minutes, Barry spoke. "I think it's safe to go in. I think the shooter has completed his mission."

"What mission is that?" Ashley asked. "We're not dead, so I don't think he has completed the job."

"Well, it's going to be uncomfortable sleeping on this concrete sidewalk all night. Neighbors will get the wrong impression. Let's go."

Barry stood. There were no additional shots. After a few seconds Ashley stood reluctantly, and they entered their apartment.

Within a few minutes, their heart rates had slowed to a normal rhythm. Barry stood to leave.

"Where are you going?" Ashley asked

"I'm going out to see if I can find the bullets that struck our building."

"You're doing no such thing. What if he's waiting to pick us off?"

"He's not going to pick us off. He won't want to attract any more attention. Neighbors have probably already called the police when they heard the shots. Do you think he's going to sit around with a rifle in his arms and wait for the police to arrive? He's long gone. He may be a criminal, but he's not stupid."

Barry got a flashlight and proceeded to the front of the building. Ashley followed. She wasn't going to let Barry have all the fun.

They found three bullet holes in the building. "How can you be so calm when somebody just tried to kill us?" Ashley asked.

"Nobody tried to kill us," Barry answered. "Look. We were standing there," pointing to the sidewalk several feet away. "The bullets struck here, probably ten feet from where we were standing. And notice this. The gunman was a pretty good shot. The cluster of bullets is within a 15 to 18 inch circle, not an easy accomplishment when you consider he was probably shooting from over there, probably 50 yards away. He wasn't trying to kill us. He doesn't want a murder charge on his hands. He was just trying to scare us. Somebody has become uncomfortable with our findings. Somebody is trying to scare us enough that we will withdraw from the case."

They dug the bullets from the apartment building's siding, being careful not to damage ballistics markings.

The following day Barry took the bullets to the police department's crime lab and asked if they would compare these bullets with those Ashley had removed from Nutley's home in Dublin.

Barry got the word later that day. The bullets removed from Barry's and Ashley's apartment building had identical ballistics signature marks with those removed from Nutley's home. A new piece of the puzzle had been put into place.

"We have been thinking that Nutley wants us out of the picture. And he probably does. Now we know Nutley didn't take shots at us last night. Someone else did," Barry summarized. "Someone else wants us out of the picture too."

"I agree," Ashley chimed in. "Whoever shot at us also shot at Nutley's house and car. We know Nutley had no reason to shoot at his own home and car thinking he might implicate others. This would only cause law enforcement people to ask more questions and to snoop around his home and his business more thoroughly. This would not be to his advantage. Somebody wants Nutley dead or out of the picture. And that same person wants us to stop our investigation. Whoever shot at us last night is probably the Big Boss we're looking for or was acting at the request of the Big Boss."

"You're right," Barry answered. "Nutley's conviction will only partially solve the problem. Someone else is calling the shots, and we're beginning to make him nervous. We've got to identify that person and bring him to justice or the 1-800 murders will continue."

17.

It was 6:30 a.m. and Howard Nutley aimed his black Lamborghini, bullet hole and all, north on I-71 toward Cleveland. He had several important clients headquartered there, and he tried to visit them periodically. They had been attracted to his investment business by his $450,000 Lamborghini, his $6,000 Armani suits, an unstinting lifestyle, and his reputation for delivering unmatched returns on investments. Capping off his profuse display of material extravagance was an extraordinary skill for schmoozing and a dazzling display of his super-sized ego. Every indication is that Nutley is a picture of unequaled success.

This visit with Cleveland clients was somewhat more critical. Nutley recognized that the tide was turning. The informal communication network among investors is an active one. There are not many secrets. Several Cleveland investors had heard the rumors that something was amiss in Nutley's investment business, and several were doing a war dance, calling even more attention to the rumors. He had to do something—right away—to salvage his business.

As usual, early morning traffic on I-71 north was fairly heavy as many businesspeople from Columbus and Cincinnati headed toward Cleveland or points in between for business meetings of some type.

Nutley cruised along slightly above the posted speed limit, about the pace of normal traffic. He had always looked for an opportunity to see what his Lamborghini would really do. When no cars were in sight, he would stop completely on the Interstate—then put the 691 horsepower V12 with the seven speed transmission to work, hitting 60 mph in less than three seconds, leaving long black streaks on the highway. But he never had an opportunity to test its 217 mph top speed. This required the exercise of the very limit of his personal discipline, but he knew the Ohio State Highway Patrol would not be forgiving.

Beyond the Mansfield exit, the terrain became rolling and hilly. As he passed by one of the most aggressive hills on the trip, with about a hundred feet drop off, a gray Chevrolet Impala pulled alongside, moved to the right, slamming into Nutley's black Lamborghini. Nutley fought the wheel trying to keep his car on the road, but it was impossible. He went over the steep embankment, rolling seven times down the sharp incline.

The gray Chevy did not stop and continued on north.

Several motorists following nearby stopped to help and called 911. Two witnesses saw the accident occur, but nobody got a license number in the near darkness and could not provide a specific description.

Nutley was banged up a bit with cuts and bruises, but he had his seat belt fastened and was not seriously injured. After the police came and a tow truck rescued his car, a Good Samaritan took him on to Cleveland where he rented a car so he could carry forth with his previously-planned client calls.

Ashley heard about the accident from Nutley's business associates in Columbus and then checked with her police department friends to see if they could shed any light on the accident.

Despite Barry's and Ashley's decision to turn their attention away from Nutley for a while, Howard Nutley just wouldn't go away. It was obvious Nutley enjoyed a flamboyant lifestyle. He may have liked Barry's and Ashley's attention too.

Two days later police were notified that a gray Chevy Impala had been abandoned in the statehouse underground garage in Columbus. The car was damaged on the right side, streaked with a healthy dose of black paint matching that of Nutley's car.

Ashley learned that the abandoned car was titled to National Rental Car. They said the car had been rented using a driver's license and credit card belonging to William Garrity of Pickerington, Ohio. Mr. Garrity told Ashley that his wallet had been lost or stolen at an Ohio State football game. Notice of the loss had been given to the credit card company, but apparently the car was rented before the notice made it through the system. Ashley believed Garrity was telling the truth and had no role in renting the car.

Within a matter of days, thanks to prompt service from his insurance company, Nutley was driving a new Lamborghini, this one bright red. Nutley took pride in his new car and was seen showing it off all over town. If he had been the least bit intimidated by the I-71 accident, it didn't show.

From outward appearances, everything in Nutley's life was normal. His investment business was thriving, his bountiful lifestyle was continuing, and he looked to have not a care in the world....until.

Until a morning two weeks later when he arrived at his office and was met by a dozen or so SEC auditors. Nutley was surprised. He hadn't expected the feds to come in this soon, and not with so many people. Had the SEC made the decision on its own to make a thorough audit of his investment business? Or did his client, Tom Brody, have the influence with the SEC to instigate the audit as he said he would?

"We have probably two weeks or more of work to do here,"

Daniel Cooper, the lead auditor, told Nutley. "We will need many of your records, and we'll have many questions for you. Don't leave town. We will need to visit with you every day as our investigation develops."

"I'm most happy to comply," Nutley answered, in his friendly sales voice and with his phony smile. "I have nothing to hide, and I'll do anything I can to be helpful. When you have completed your audit, I'm sure you will find everything is in order. Just let me know what I can do to help you."

At lunchtime Nutley left the building, telling the auditors and his administrative assistant he was leaving for lunch at Bob Evans and would be back shortly. He went to the bank and withdrew $500,000. He wanted a million but the bank couldn't accommodate a request for this much cash on such short notice.

He dropped by his home, packed a bag and headed south.

Later that afternoon Ashley heard from Nutley's associates that he had not returned from lunch. Yet no one was concerned. It wasn't that unusual for Nutley to change his schedule at the last minute, often without informing anyone. It was two days later before his absence stirred concerns.

Barry and Ashley filled in the police department with the circumstantial evidence they had gathered about Nutley's possible involvement with murders in Pittsburgh, Kansas City, Denver and St. Louis. Possible guilt seems amplified by his sudden disappearance.

The department brought in the FBI, and an APB was issued naming Nutley as a person of interest in connection with a murder investigation.

Ashley and Barry expected quick results. After all, a red

Lamborghini shouldn't be that hard to find. But nothing happened for more than a week when police in Key West reported a red Lamborghini, bearing a license plate issued to Howard Nutley, had been abandoned at a local hotel. Nutley, however, was not to be found. He had checked out of the hotel, and Key West police could not find him registered at other hotels on the island. This is not to say he wasn't still in Key West. It's just that police had not seen anyone matching his description.

"Why would someone abandon a half million dollar car?" Barry asked.

"He didn't have a lot to lose," Ashley answered. "The car was leased. Also, I've found he's five months behind on the payments on his three million dollar Dublin mansion. It's obvious his personal fortunes, as well as his business fortunes, are crumbing. He isn't walking away from very much."

Several days passed. Still no Howard Nutley. Then police in Fort Myers reported a person resembling Nutley may have disembarked from the Big Cat Catamaran that operates between Key West and Fort Myers Beach. It's a high speed, jet powered, shuttle that makes the trip in just four hours. Fort Myers police emailed the man's picture recorded by security cameras.

Certainly the man's height and build matched that of Nutley. He had the same mannerisms—walked straight and tall, his chin up, an air of superiority. But the man in the picture wore a baseball cap, sun glasses and sported a several-day-old stubble. The picture may have been of Nutley, but positive identification was not possible.

Weeks passed and Howard Nutley is still on the loose. Nutley appears to be a man who has walked away from his home, his car, his job, his career, and his life. That leaves the possibility of a murderer wandering the streets who might show his hand at any time.

Barry and Ashley know they have not seen the last of Howard Nutley. Their only question is when and where his footprints will show up next.

18.

It was shortly before lunch when Barry's and Ashley's phone rang. "This is Mike Moseley. My staff and I are in the midst of putting today's program together, and this just came over the wire. The murders are solved. Two brothers—Lewis and Perry Pixley—have confessed. It doesn't look like we will need your services any longer. It looks like this whole bad picture show is behind us."

Barry and Ashley checked all the wire stories on the Internet.

According to wire reports, two brothers—Lewis and Perry Pixley—were serving life sentences at the Northern Correction Institution at Somers, Connecticut. Northern Correctional houses male death row inmates serving long sentences for violent crimes. The Pixleys had murdered a family of two adults and two children in Springfield 16 months earlier.

The brothers reportedly became seriously ill, did not respond to treatments by prison medical personnel, and were being transported by van to a medical center in Hartford. The inmates somehow freed themselves from restraints, kicked open the van doors, and jumped from the van traveling at more than 60 mph. When the two corrections officers in the van heard the commotion, they pulled the van to the side of the highway and took shots at the escaping inmates. Chase dogs and a helicopter search failed to locate the escapees.

More than a dozen stolen cars were involved in the cross-country chase, the inmates abandoning one stolen car a few hours after it was stolen and then stealing another. Police were always behind times on what car they were looking for.

From Connecticut, the Pixleys went on a multi-state murder rampage, claiming to murder innocent people in at least nine cities. Their violence spree ended in Austin, Texas, where law enforcement people apprehended the brothers as they tried to steal a car in an Austin parking garage. They are being held in the Travis County State Jail.

Ashley and Barry traced the series of murders based on news accounts.

The first was in Philadelphia where the brothers confessed to killing a couple who was returning home from a shopping trip. They had parked their car in their garage, opened the trunk to unload groceries, when the couple was shot. Money was taken from the lady's purse, money and a Visa card were taken from the man's wallet, and their car stolen. The lady's diamond ring and expensive watch were not taken. The credit card was used about two hours later to buy gasoline and food. It was not used after that.

The next stop, according to their confession, was in Pittsburgh where they killed an elderly man in his home. Nothing was stolen.

Based on the time line Barry and Ashley were preparing, considering the time of the escape and the time of the Philadelphia murder, the Pixley brothers could have been in Pittsburgh at the time of the murder.

But the Kansas City murder didn't fit. "Nearly two weeks had passed since the Pittsburgh murder," Ashley noted. "What were they doing for two weeks? People on the run tend to be on the run. They're not comfortable lounging around for very long. No one reported seeing them over that period. No crimes in which they might have been involved were reported. This is strange."

The Denver murder fit the timeline somewhat better. The victim was elderly. He lived alone. But, again, no money or credit cards were taken, nothing was stolen from the home nor was there any damage, and the car was not stolen.

The next confessed murder was in Salt Lake City. Then Las Vegas. Back to St. Louis.

"Why would they retrace their steps from Las Vegas back to St. Louis?" Barry asked. "Also, the stolen cars attributed to the Pixleys don't correspond to the murder sites. The pieces don't fit together."

A week after the St. Louis murder, the brothers confessed to a murder in Oklahoma City—a single mother who was leaving her place of employment just after dark. She was beaten repeatedly with a blunt object such as a steel pipe or jack handle; her money and credit card were stolen; and her car was taken. The credit card was used only once and that was to buy gasoline and food.

The final stop in the brothers' killing spree was in Austin where they were apprehended while trying to steal a car. No murder was attributed to them in Austin. Police said they were apprehended before they had time to kill again.

Barry and Ashley continued to read the news reports developed from local sources and talked to police in each of the cities where the brothers confessed to murders. Every new piece of information was placed in the proper position on the time line.

"Much of this doesn't fit," Barry exclaimed. "There's more to the Pixley puzzle than appears on the surface. We've got some work to do."

Barry called the authorities in Austin and received

permission to interview the Pixleys. Barry boarded a plane in Columbus, to Midway Chicago, then on to Austin.

Lewis and Perry Pixley were anxious to talk. They smiled, and chatted, often with one interrupting the other. They liked the attention they were getting. They appeared to be proud of their accomplishments. Their life-long dream was being fulfilled. They were celebrities.

19.

It was nearly impossible to schedule an appointment with Mike Moseley during the morning hours. He and his staff were at work by 7 a.m. or earlier reviewing political developments over the past 24 hours and doing research on topics that might be discussed on today's *Tomorrow* program. Barry and Ashley were escorted to the radio station's conference room just prior to 4 p.m., just as his three-hour program ended, and they heard the last few minutes of today's program.

"I paid $4.11 a gallon for gasoline today," a caller complained. "Driving is a part of my job. I can't make a living without using my pickup truck. The oil companies are driving me out of business. I think it's time for the federal government to take over the oil companies."

"Gasoline is too expensive. There's no argument there. But many of the cost problems are caused by government, not the oil companies. Permit me to break down the cost for you.

"First is the cost of the crude oil. That amounts to 76% of the cost of a gallon of gas. This portion of the cost is controlled primarily by global oil cartels. How can we reduce this portion of the cost? Drill more in America. We have fuel sources in this country which could be used if the government would allow oil companies to drill on government-controlled land.

"Next, the oil has to be refined. It has to be converted into a form your pickup truck can use. This conversion process amounts to 6% of the cost of a gallon of gasoline.

"Next is distribution. Gas has to be shipped to distribution centers and then transported to your local gasoline station. That's another 6% added to the cost.

"Now the fun part. The remaining 12% is taxes—federal and state. The federal tax currently amounts to 18.4 cents per gallon. State taxes vary from a low of 8 cents per gallon in Alaska to 49 cents in New York and 48.6 cents in California and Connecticut. The other states are somewhere in between.

"What do you think is a reasonable profit for oil companies?"

"Are you talking to me?"

"Yes, I'm talking to you. Do you think seven cents a gallon is a reasonable profit for the oil companies?"

"Yes, I think that's fair."

"That's exactly the situation. Last year Exxon made seven cents a gallon, a modest return for millions and millions of dollars of investments and substantial risk; and the federal, state and local governments made 50 cents a gallon, with no risk and no investment.

"I don't know about you, but I like the odds of having my gasoline provided by oil companies that are competing for my business. If government gets into the oil business, there is no competition to keep it in line.

"If you want to do something about the high cost of gasoline, write to your congress people to encourage their support of more exploration and drilling on federal lands. Politicians say oil production is up, and it is. Production on privately owned lands has grown rapidly, but production on federal lands dropped 23% between 2010 and 2012. The same, incidentally, is true with natural gas. Production on privately owned lands has grown by 40% since 2007, while production on government lands has fallen by 33%.

"Also encourage the government to permit the building of additional refineries. The environmentalists have been holding this up for years. Then let competitive forces work to keep prices down. Competition works. When services are provided by government, there are no competitive forces to keep prices down and, in fact, no incentive to deliver services efficiently."

Moseley's program came to a close, and he and Zack Forrester came into the conference room.

"I suppose you have a bill for us," station manager Forrester said.

"Frankly, we don't," Barry answered.

"Why not? The murderer has confessed. There's nothing further for you to do."

"I just returned from Austin," Barry answered, "and I interviewed Lewis and Perry Pixley. I'm one hundred percent certain they did not commit the murders we have been investigating."

"They confessed."

"Yes, I know they confessed," Barry went on, "but they didn't commit the murders. False confessions aren't a new phenomenon. They have been happening for years. More than 200 people confessed to kidnapping Charles Lindbergh's baby in 1932. Dozens confessed to killing O. J. Simpson's estranged wife Nicole Brown Simpson. Toll-free crime hot lines are jammed with calls from people confessing to unsolved crimes. False confessions may play a role in as many as 25% of all crimes. And murder suspects are at the top of the list."

"Why would they want to do that?"

"Psychologists have been trying to figure this out for years. Some are mentally impaired or are young and easily led by persistent interrogators. Others want attention or sympathy.

Or they want their moment in the spotlight. They may have a pathological need for notoriety.

"In the case of the Pixley brothers, I believe it is the latter.

"Lewis and Perry Pixley consider themselves celebrities. They love to talk about it, and they are proud of their accomplishments. They love the headlines. And they feel they have nothing to lose. They were serving life sentences for murder. Throw in a prison escape and a few more murders, they'll be right back where they were with life sentences plus the celebrity glow of Bonnie and Clyde."

"What makes you think they didn't commit the murders?"

"They claim to have committed nine murders, although only eight can be verified. They can't name the ninth. They may have committed the murder in Philadelphia—a couple returning from the grocery store. They stole money, a credit card, and a car. There's a chance they committed the murder in Oklahoma City. The mode of operation was entirely different for these murders.

"They had knowledge of the murders in Pittsburgh, Kansas City, Denver, and St. Louis. But the only thing they knew about the murders is precisely what they read in the newspapers.

"They didn't know the parts of town in which the victims lived. They knew nothing about the ages of the victims; they didn't know if family members were in the home; they didn't know in what part of the body the bullet struck; they didn't know how many shots were fired; they didn't know what type of weapon was used; they didn't know that different weapons were used. The only thing they knew was what was in the newspapers and on TV.

"Although I didn't specifically mention the inscriptions on the victims' foreheads, I led them far enough along to know they knew nothing about it. And they are as apolitical as anyone I've ever talked to. They are neither conservative nor liberal. Their political persuasion might be called prisoncratic. They know prison politics, but that's all. They have no interest in the political system in the real world.

"When I asked them why they had committed the murders, both shrugged and finally Perry answered, 'Because they were there.'"

"We've talked to the police in each of the cities where the Pixley murders are alleged, and they have a list of suspects," Ashley added. "They too have reservations about Pixleys' confession. One murder was committed with a steel bar. The others by hand gun. They are doing ballistics checks now that will shed more light on the matter, but we know the Pixleys are not involved in the four murders we are investigating."

"So your work is not done?" Moseley asked.

"Not unless you want us to stop midstream," Barry answered. "We believe the Pixley brothers are nothing more than a short-term distraction. We think we're 80 percent of the way toward solving the *Tomorrow* murders—maybe even 90 percent. We have several additional leads we don't feel comfortable talking about right now. We don't have sufficient evidence to support a conclusion. Maybe it's more of a hunch than corroborating evidence, but we're confident it's worth checking out."

"How much longer will this be going on?" Forrester asked. "We want to keep the expenses associated with your investigation as low as possible."

"If we don't have it tied down firmly in two weeks—with solid evidence that will support charges that will hold up in court—we'll finish the job at no cost to you."

"That sounds fair enough," Moseley answered.

20.

He entered the WBEO studios and asked to speak to Mike Moseley.

"Do you have an appointment?" the receptionist asked.

"No. I don't have an appointment. I have a business matter to discuss."

"Mr. Moseley is on the air right now. I'm not sure he will have time to talk to you today. He has a very busy schedule."

"Of course. I know he's on the air right now. I can hear him. Any idiot would know that."

"I'll check to see if he has time to see you today. If he can work you into his schedule, it will be more than an hour before his program ends. You'll have to wait."

"If I have to wait, I suppose I'll wait," the man said rudely.

The receptionist placed a note on Moseley's console during a commercial break telling him a very ill-mannered man is waiting to talk to him. Moseley frowned and said, "OK, after 4."

"Mr. Moseley said he could see you for a few minutes. Please be seated. He will be out shortly after four."

The man sat and listened to Mike's program on the reception area's speaker for about ten minutes. He fidgeted while wringing his hands. He looked at his watch. It was obvious he didn't like the conversation he was hearing. Again, he looked at his watch and stepped outside. He walked back and forth in front of the studios, checking his watch every minute or so.

After his program came to a close, Moseley came to the reception area and greeted the man. "It's about time," he said rudely. Mike escorted him to the conference room.

"My name is Bruce Fogleman," he said to Moseley. "I'm with the Washington, D. C. law firm of Flint, Gardner, Klein and Fogleman. You're going to be glad you are seeing me today. I want to talk to you about a very lucrative business proposition I'm confident you will like."

The man looked determined—a man who was not prepared to take no for an answer. He was about six feet two, 195 pounds, dark hair, wearing an expensive dark pin-striped suit, well-shined shoes, and a tie that cost more than most of Moseley's suits. His face was punctuated with a thin, straight, closely-clipped pencil-style mustache, coal black. With his slicked down hair, he could have been cast as a body guard for Al Capone.

"Well, I'm involved with my own lucrative business deal that I'm pretty happy with. I can't imagine I'd be interested in anything else right now, but I'm willing to hear you out. Tell me what you have in mind."

"Our firm has a client that would like to employ you in a capacity you will find most attractive."

"Employ me to do what?"

"You would be my client's public relations person."

"The term public relations covers a lot of territory. Specifically what would my activities encompass?"

"No specific job description has been prepared at this time, but I would say it generally involves being a spokesperson for my client when called upon."

"Who might your client be?"

"We're not at liberty to discuss that at this time."

"I'm certainly not interested in being a spokesperson for a client who cannot be identified."

"You may feel differently when I tell you about your

compensation arrangements. My client is willing to sign a five year contract paying you $1.5 million a year, plus expenses, with an option to renew for another five years."

"Compensation is not a topic of discussion unless I know who the client is and what is expected of me. Do you think I would be willing to be a spokesperson for Enron, regardless of compensation? I might as well be the PR guy for John Dillinger. This is something you probably can't relate to, but I live my life by a set of principles. I don't care if the compensation is $1.5 million a year, $3 million, $5 million or $10 million. If my livelihood isn't consistent with those principles that are important to me, I'm simply not going to do it. I'd rather be a parking lot attendant at minimum wage."

"My client is actually several clients—a group of people—very important people. If you will seriously consider my offer, I'm willing to divulge the names of my clients upon your signing a non-disclosure agreement."

"My duties would have to be more specifically defined. Although I make speeches around the country from time to time, for the most part I'm here—I'm home—with my family—where I want to be. If my duties require that I be on the road seven days a week, I'm not interested, regardless of the compensation"

"I can assure you, your duties would not require you to be on the road seven days a week. Nor five days a week. Not even two or three days a week. We're willing to make that a part of the contract."

"If my duties require so little time, then I suppose you would not mind if I continued my radio program or performed other work outside of that required by my new employer?"

"On this my clients will not negotiate. Your contract will

contain a non-compete clause which will state that you cannot make public statements inconsistent with a set of guidelines set forth by my clients."

"My suggestion is that you find someone else to do your work. I can name a dozen others who can do the job very effectively."

"Actually, this offer is being made to five of you countrywide. All five of you will be regional public relations representatives with identical job requirements. In fact, my clients are making it mandatory that all five of you agree to the new contract before we can make the offers final."

"I don't understand. It's five or nothing? What do the five of us have in common?"

"All five of you are popular radio talk show hosts. My clients believe all five of you have a great deal of credibility with the American people, and they believe America will be better served if all of you become spokespeople for new interests and for a different political agenda."

"So you're saying you want all five of us off the air?"

"That's a crude way of saying it. We would prefer to say we would like your influence redirected."

"This is probably also a crude way of saying it, but I say you can go stick it."

"We know you are a very persistent person, Mr. Moseley, but my clients are equally persistent, if not even more persistent. They insist on getting the results they want, one way or the other."

"This means getting rough if they have to?"

"It depends on what you mean by getting rough. I can assure you they will get what they want in the end. Neither you nor anyone else will stand in their way. Frankly, Mr. Moseley, I like you, and I want to give you every opportunity to go along with this very lucrative business opportunity. I am authorized to go up to $1.75 million a year."

"What I said earlier still holds true. I have my principles which I will not violate."

"My final offer--$2 million a year. And the contract will extend for a period of ten years."

"I wouldn't think of getting my hands dirty with your money. It's a flat no."

"I'm sorry you have taken a hard-line approach, Mr. Moseley. I can tell you the time will come when you will wish you had accepted my generous offer."

"Is that a threat?"

"Interpret it as you choose, Mr. Moseley." As Fogleman stood to leave, he added, "It was a pleasure meeting a person of such great prestige and influence. I'm sure we will be meeting again soon."

Moseley couldn't wait to call Barry and Ashley and fill them in on Fogleman's visit and the offer he laid out. "Even had I liked the deal, I didn't trust Fogleman. Webster should have this guy's picture next to the word 'shyster.'"

"Do you know who the other four persons are who have been offered the contract?" Barry asked.

"The only thing he acknowledged is they are all radio talk show hosts. I would assume they are the most popular conservative talk show hosts in the country, but he didn't name them."

"You know most of the others in the conservative talk show business. Do you think any of them will go along with Fogleman's deal?" Ashley asked.

"This guy couldn't sell a life preserver to a drowning man. Although I suppose I'm biased, I think the conservative talk show folks are pretty bright, too bright to fall for this scheme. I wouldn't trust Fogleman to draft a will for my dog. Then the conversation ended with a threat."

"Enough of a threat that his clients might consider murder?" Barry asked.

"I wouldn't be all that surprised. If they are willing to spend $2 million a year, for each of five radio talk show hosts, for five or ten years, they are talking about real money. For an investment of that size, they are expecting to eliminate a major conservative influence in our country. If they can't buy themselves this change, I think they might be willing to do whatever they have to do to get the results they want."

"Does this mean another name should be added to our suspect list?" Ashley asked.

"I think so. I think these people have the ability to play rough. Very rough."

21.

"Do you know of a law firm in your town called Flint, Gardner, Klein and Fogleman?" Barry was on the phone with Jeremy Diehl, a Washington, D. C. private investigator who had worked with Barry and Ashley on another case.

"I don't know them personally, but their reputation is well known. They are hot shots in political circles. They call themselves lobbyists, and they also refer to themselves as a commercial research firm. By calling a good portion of their staff researchers, they get around legal licensing requirements. They work primarily with campaigns of far-left politicians."

"What about a lawyer named Bruce Fogleman?"

"He's probably the most legitimate one of the bunch, but that's not saying much. If you could put all the lawyers in the country in a barrel and shake it up, Fogleman and his cronies would sink to the bottom in about ten seconds. I wouldn't trust this crew with my lunch money. What's your interest in this outfit?"

"They represent clients who want our client to give up his conservative radio talk show. Apparently they don't want the public to get a conservative perspective on any issue."

"That sounds like this bunch. They want to shut down anyone who might not support their liberal clients."

"Why now?" Barry asked. "The next election is more than three years away."

"Electioneering is a full-time operation in this town. Before the polls closed in 2012, Fogleman and his beltway buddies were preparing the way for 2016. And even 2020."

"Do you know the names of some of their clients?"

"It's fairly well known in political circles that their primary clients are the campaign organizations of several U. S. Senators. They don't advertise it as such, but there is no question these are the clients to which they devote most of their time. I'm told they also do some work for some lesser candidates—a few House members and some governors. But the U. S. Senators generate the real bucks."

"I guess I understand their mission. But does this just involve buying-off people who have a different perspective?"

"No, they employ a number of tactics, most of which you never hear about on the eleven o'clock news. They have employees as well as independent contractor arrangements with a great many low-life goons who dig up dirt on political opponents or supporters of opponents."

"This is a dimension of the political world I'm not familiar with," Barry said. "Like what?"

"Like rummaging through the personal lives of opponents to find something that might be embarrassing, from grade school on."

"I've heard about politicians going through the trash of an opponent, but I thought that was an overstatement. This really occurs?"

"Yes, it really occurs. There are people in these United States who make their living doing just that. They talk to former teachers, neighbors, business associates, and, yes, the trash man, and anyone else they can find who might have, or have had, a remote relationship with the opponent. It's easy to find someone to say something negative, for all of us have had someone in our lives who doesn't like us. Once they find a comment or an issue that may not be totally popular politically, they will use that statement to organize a smear campaign. It doesn't necessarily have to be the truth.

It's OK to distort the truth a bit. News reporters tend to be lazy. They live on news releases. If someone puts out a news release saying that Opponent A doesn't like dogs, it tends to get printed. And if the issue is repeated often enough, it becomes the truth, and the general public believes Opponent A mistreats puppies.

"If the opponent got a D in high school, the release might say—'Here's a person who wants to represent you in Congress and help determine tax rates and financial policy, and she got a D in math. Is that the kind of person you want to vote for?' That's the kind of thing their so-called professional researchers look for."

"I guess that's one of the reasons politicians are rated more poorly than lice, brussels sprouts, colonoscopies, and root canals."

"It gets even worse. If you run for public office, I suppose you can expect attacks like these. But these people also attack donors."

"Donors? You've got to be kidding."

"I'm afraid not. If someone, say in California, Texas or elsewhere, has made a hundred thousand dollar contribution to an opponent, one or more of Fogleman's thugs will be assigned to dig up dirt on the donor. In one case a donor's wife had made a contribution to an anti-gay-marriage campaign a dozen or so years ago. This became a campaign issue.

"If the donor has been divorced, or involved in business lawsuits, or has supported controversial causes, they check court records and other sources to look for anything that might be embarrassing. Then they encourage customers to call and harass business owners. They ask shoppers not to buy at their businesses. Many get death threats, although we don't know if this is done by Fogleman's people or whether the public is responding to negative publicity. When this occurs, major donors tend not to give more money, and those who might consider making donations are reluctant to do so.

"Some politicians claim to support full disclosure of campaign contributors, implying that this will somehow clean up the campaign cesspool. Actually, their real purpose is to get names of the opponents' donors so Fogleman's professional researchers and others like them can trash their reputations."

"I guess I knew politics was a sleazy business. I just didn't think it was this sleazy. I don't understand how they get away with it."

"In this town you can get away with murder if you represent a left-wing viewpoint."

"Really? Murder?"

"I meant that as a figure of speech. But, yes, maybe even murder. Most of us have never known personally anyone who has been murdered. In political circles, however, there are many examples in which associates have been murdered. Yet law enforcement and the media never connect the two. It's a hand-off situation."

"You have given me a new perspective on the world of politics. I had thought it was criminal enough to lie during a campaign. Politicians campaign on a set of principles they claim to believe in, but their philosophies shift 180 degrees once elected. Many of them couldn't tell the truth if their tongues were notarized."

"I agree. The country would be in far better shape if voters paid no attention to what is said during a campaign. What a politician says during the campaign seldom reflects on his or her actions once elected. The only way to evaluate a politician, or anyone else for that matter, is to evaluate what they have done in the past. Their past is the only accurate indicator of what they will likely do in the future. The American people should stop paying for expensive, worthless campaigns that don't shed light on the real person. But don't expect improved ethics in politics anytime soon. They will be dribbling footballs before common sense changes will be made in political campaigns."

"Seriously," Barry went on, "if you were involved in a murder investigation affecting a person who espouses a conservative political philosophy, you really believe someone like Fogleman might be involved?"

"Don't rule them out. Their paid thugs will do whatever it takes to win an election. Ethics don't matter. And criminal activity doesn't matter. Only winning matters."

22.

Mike Moseley phoned Barry's and Ashley's office. Ashley answered.

"I've got bad news, I'm afraid," Moseley began. "It looks like we have another murder on our hands. This one is in Indianapolis. It looks like you were right about the Pixley brothers. We understand they are still in custody in Austin."

"How did you learn about it?" Ashley asked.

"A caller to my show told us about it. It was all over the local paper in Indianapolis. Herb took the call and alerted me. We didn't put the caller on the air."

"We will check it out with the Indianapolis police," Ashley answered. "That's not a long drive, so we'll go over and check it out in person." Ashley hesitated for a few seconds and went on. "It's interesting that Herb is passing along this information. Does this mean Herb is trying to divert attention from himself by being overly cooperative, or does it mean he is totally innocent?"

"Herb and I have been working together closely for six years. Although Herb's political philosophies and mine are 180 degrees apart, I have never for a minute distrusted him. I do not believe Herb is involved in providing caller information to a murderer or is otherwise directing the operation."

"I understand why you might feel that way," Ashley answered. "But you tend to give people the benefit of the doubt. You see the good in everyone, whether or not they agree with your positions.

"I think Herb's cooperation paints a more positive picture

than a negative one," Ashley went on, "but we see all types of reactions from people who are as guilty as sin. Some people have the ability to conceal their guilt very well. Sooner or later the truth comes out, as it will with Herb, but as this point we can't take any name off the table. I think our case is going together pretty well. We should have the answer soon."

Barry and Ashley left for Indianapolis. The murder encompassed similar MOs as the other murders they had investigated.

The victim lived alone. There was no forcible entry and no evidence of struggles of any type. The victim either knew the intruder or felt comfortable that the murderer posed no danger.

The victim was politically conservative. Unlike the other victims, however, he was not reluctant to share his views with others. All his friends and neighbors were subjected to a steady stream of comments about how this country is headed toward ruin if we don't get our debt, deficit and political corruption under control. Interestingly, however, most of his friends and neighbors shared his views. No one appeared to be upset with the victim because of his views, and most, in fact, were even more vocal about the country's unsustainable spending and debt and its dramatic shift toward socialism.

The victim listened to Moseley's *Tomorrow* radio program, and a review of program tapes confirmed he had called the program.

Ballistics shows that the gun used in the murder was not the same one used in the other four murders.

There were no fingerprints or DNA left at the scene. The same type of disinfectant had been used to wipe doorknobs, arms of chairs, and anything else the murderer may have touched. This would seem to indicate the same murderer is at work.

No strange cars or unusual activity had been noted by neighbors. It's a quiet neighborhood where there is little crime and everybody knows everybody else. In these low-crime communities, people tend not to be especially watchful or suspicious of others. There is no need to do so. Nothing ever happens here.

All these points were similarities, which could and should point to the same murderer. But there was a major dissimilarity as well that created further question about the identity of the murderer.

The word *2morrow* had been inked on the forehead of the victim, just as had been the case with the other four murders. But the graphologist employed by Ashley and Barry is 99% certain the word was written by a different person, based on form, style, slant, pressure, spacing, and the like. All the other characteristics followed the pattern of the earlier murders.

"Up to this point, all evidence has led to Howard Nutley," Ashley said. "Now, because of the handwriting dissimilarity, we can't be so sure. Our investigation has been set back for a few days."

"Also," Barry added, "this is the first murder that didn't take place on a Thursday or Friday. This one occurred on a Tuesday. Now that Nutley doesn't appear to have a job or other demands on his time, he can commit murder any day of the week. But the handwriting issue creates a degree of uncertainty."

"Even if we had our mitts on Nutley right now, very likely we couldn't make a charge stick," Ashley answered, "for our evidence isn't strong enough. Our only hope is to find good DNA that could make a murder charge stick. But, of course, there's a chance Nutley would sing like a canary, putting all the pieces together for us, implicating his associate or associates, and help us put the case to bed. The fact that Nutley's on the run is a good sign. He's either afraid of us, or he's afraid of the SEC accountants, or both. If the APB guides police to him, he may be more willing to cooperate than we think."

23.

"Ashley, come here! Quick!" Barry called to Ashley as she was preparing dinner and Barry was reading the paper while giving scant attention to TV news.

By the time Ashley made it into the family room, the TV news story Barry had noted was long past. Americans get their information in ten second sound bites, which is why most people are ill informed. A ten second news story can deliver adequate news on an auto accident or a house fire, but it can't interpret significant events or major legislation that might intimately affect every family. The American people live on an information diet of sound bites.

"What is it?" Ashley asked.

"I'm not sure, but I think I just saw Howard Nutley on TV. It had something to do with a GAFF meeting someplace. Maybe in Las Vegas."

But Barry wasn't certain. The news story had passed by quickly, and Barry had been concentrating more fully on the newspaper than on TV news.

"I would swear it was Nutley, but I want to make sure. Let's go to Channel 4 tomorrow morning and take a look at the tape of the newscast."

Station personnel happily complied with their request. The story, eight seconds in length, was an interview with Carl Bristol, the national chairman of GAFF and the speaker at a meeting of a newly formed chapter in Las Vegas. Bristol said they are expecting a big turnout for the first meeting of the Las Vegas chapter and they are well on their way to making GAFF the largest progressive activist organization in America.

The TV image looked like Nutley. He sounded like Nutley. His mannerisms were that of Nutley. Both Ashley and Barry are confident this is the Howard Nutley they've been looking for, now using the Carl Bristol alias.

"I remember Carl Bristol," Ashley said. "Carl Bristol is the one who rented a car while trailing me in Pittsburgh. At any rate, that was the name on the rental agreement.

"When I returned to Columbus, I checked it out and found the street address didn't exist and that no Carl Bristol had rented a car in Pittsburgh. Nutley is now working under his assumed name. We know he has a driver's license and credit card with that name. He probably has other forms of identification as well. Police have been looking for Howard Nutley when they should be looking for Carl Bristol."

"It looks like the new Howard Nutley is now devoting his full attention to his liberal passion of promoting the GAFF agenda," Barry added, "with a new name and identity. Before he left town, he had an extraordinary interest in GAFF. Now that he is not bogged down with the management of other people's money, he can devote his full attention to liberal causes."

"Perhaps he's giving full attention to GAFF," Ashley said. "Or he may still be a part-time murderer of people who hold conservative views. Let's not forget his probable involvement with four murders and possibly a fifth."

The Channel 4 people gave Barry and Ashley a DVD of the news item which they took to the police department. "Take a look at this," Barry said. "Here's the Howard Nutley you and the FBI have been looking for. He now calls himself Carl Bristol."

A new APB was issued listing his Carl Bristol alias, noting he had last been seen in Las Vegas.

Reports came back from the Las Vegas police that Carl Bristol had checked out of the hotel at which he had been registered, and police are nearly certain he has moved on.

"There's got to be a newsletter, or some type of communication, that lists GAFF meetings across the country, especially newly formed chapters. If we can find a schedule of events, police will know where to look," Ashley said. "Now we just have to find a GAFF member who will cooperate with us."

"Let's ask Herb," Barry answered. "He has been especially forthcoming about calls that come into the station. He knows that we know he is a part of the local GAFF group. Let's see if he is willing to help us take a step toward finding Nutley, or Bristol."

Herb couldn't have been more helpful when Barry approached him. Although GAFF didn't have a paper newsletter as far as Herb knew, they did have a Web site that summarized the activities of the organization and listed upcoming meetings across the country.

Ashley printed off the meeting dates and places for the next couple of months.

"Look at this," Ashley said. "Nutley, or Bristol, is not going to be overly captivated with regular meetings of local groups. A local meeting is not going to do much to further enhance his inflated ego. But the formation of new chapters and regional meetings will more likely give his already-inflated ego a huge boost. Here is a five-state regional meeting in New Orleans coming up next week. This is right down Nutley's alley."

"Good thinking," Ashley. "It should be worth our time if we plan a little welcoming party to greet Mr. Nutley when he arrives at the meeting."

24.

Barry and Dennis Connor, an FBI agent assigned to accompany Barry, showed up at the Omni Royal Orleans Hotel for the regional meeting of GAFF. The Omni Royal, about a block from Bourbon Street and near Jackson Square and the Mississippi River, was decorated with antique style furnishings and gilded wallpaper, just the kind of ambiance GAFF members believe they deserve.

Their first obstacle came when they showed up for the meeting without name tags and with no advance registration and were denied admission.

"Sorry we didn't notify you," Barry said confidently. "We are from the press, and we're anxious to tell the GAFF story to our readers. But if you prefer to get no publicity...."

"Oh no," a GAFF leader replied. "We'll be glad to find a place for you." He was the person at the door who seemed most important—the one who had the greatest authority.

Barry and Agent Connor were escorted to front row seats. Obviously GAFF was anxious to get publicity for its liberal agenda. Barry had hoped to be able to melt into the crowd and not attract attention, but they were not in a position to turn down priority seating.

The room was set up to seat about 500 people. There was a platform, about two feet high, across the front of the room with a lectern and head table for ten people.

When the 8 o'clock meeting time arrived, the master of ceremonies called the meeting to order and asked the attendees, still clustered and chattering around the room, to please take their seats.

After the majority of people had been seated, the MC began. "Good evening, ladies and gentlemen, and welcome to this first five-state regional meeting of Government Affording a Fair Future. It's so good to have you with us this evening. Some exciting things are in store with GAFF, and we're confident you will be pleased and excited to be a part of this worthwhile movement. Our purpose is to transform this country into one in which people come first, not giant corporations or special interests."

The MC failed to acknowledge that GAFF itself is a special interest group. Politicians and the media decry special interests as if they were sinful, but every single person is a member of several special interest groups—member of a certain church, a certain occupation, a special place of residence, a certain income group, and dozens of other categories—all special interests.

"I'm Conrad Walsh, president of the New Orleans chapter of GAFF and your host for this five-state regional event."

Of the ten seats at the head table, eight were filled—all male, all wearing suits and ties, and all looking very official. A chair on one side of the lectern was obviously for the master of ceremonies, Mr. Walsh. The other must have been for Nutley, but Nutley hadn't yet appeared.

"During the course of this evening," Walsh continued, "you will hear about plans to make GAFF the largest and most influential political activist organization in the United States, and you will hear from a number of chapter leaders about what they're doing to become a stronger voice in shaping legislation and government programs that are consistent with the views of our members.

"Carl Bristol, our national chairman and keynote speaker, is in town and had planned to be with us this evening. Unfortunately, he called just a few minutes ago and told us he is not feeling well and will not be able to be here. Although we are all disappointed, still we have a number of our leaders with us who are prepared to share their success stories with you. In the meantime, we extend to Mr. Bristol our best wishes for his rapid recovery."

Barry and FBI Agent Connor sat through the first three speakers, all presidents of local chapters. Their messages were nearly identical—how they had picketed campaign stops by conservative politicians and how they had showed force by gathering together homeless people, radical students, and other left-leaners, enticing them with food and cash. The program listed 17 speakers, counting Bristol. Based on the first three speakers, Barry doubted that many attendees would stick it out for the night. Bourbon Street would be far more alluring than listening to folks who probably hadn't spoken before a group since a speech class during their junior year in high school.

Being seated in the front row, it was not easy to make a graceful exit, but they felt they were wasting their time in the meeting. As they left the room, the man who had given them priority front-row seating asked, "Leaving so soon?"

"We have a deadline for the 11 o'clock news," Barry answered. The man seemed satisfied.

Barry and Connor speculated as to why Nutley had not shown up for the meeting. Was he really ill? Had he seen Barry seated in the front row and decided to skip town? Had he recognized Barry's companion as an FBI agent? FBI agents tend to dress like FBI agents. Connor was no exception. His dark blue suit shouted FBI to anyone with knowledge of law enforcement people.

"I would suspect that Mr. Nutley saw us from back stage and decided he would be better off if he suddenly came down with some form of illness," Barry said. "You can bet he'll do anything possible to kick the penalty can down the road as far as possible."

"Then too," Agent Connor continued, "Nutley has become popular with a number of people. SEC auditors cannot be too happy about his skipping town. They may have their own investigators out looking for him.

"And we know many of his investors are no longer having a love affair with him, and you can't blame them. When they find they've been duped out of millions of dollars of their savings, their trust and confidence will erode in a flash. With the amounts of money at stake, the investors could be taking the law into their own hands."

Barry and Agent Connor went to the police department and asked if they could help them find Nutley/Bristol. The police checked 75 of the more popular hotels along with a handful of B&B's. Nobody named Nutley or Bristol had been registered. Since the MC had said Bristol is in town, they suspect he may be operating under still another alias.

Although Barry and Connor are disappointed their trip to New Orleans didn't pay off immediately, some good may come of it. Nutley knows he is being pursued. When criminals become scared, they tend to make more mistakes. Both feel the Nutley saga will end soon.

25.

While Barry was in New Orleans, Ashley wasn't sitting on her hands. She had become more and more convinced Herb Bentley had not been giving caller information to a murderer. Bentley had cooperated 110% with their investigation. Ashley's assessment is that Bentley is an all-around nice guy who would not stoop to any form of lawlessness. Of course, her impression could be wrong, so she decided to check it out thoroughly so one name could be removed from the suspect list.

His bank records showed no unusual transfers, either in or out. He was not a registered owner of a firearm of any type and was not a member of NRA or any gun-owners' association. He lived within his income. Nothing stood out as being unusual.

Phone records should be more telling. Until 2006 phone records could be easily obtained by private investigators or nearly anyone with a credit card, an Internet connection, and $100. Following the Hewlett Packard scandal in 2006, when the board hired private investigators to find out who leaked confidential information to the press, the Telephone Records and Privacy Protection Act of 2006 was signed into law.

Even under the law, private investigators can obtain a court order to check on calls to or from a specific number as long as there is a valid reason to request the record and the request is not being made under false pretext. Since the murder victims had not put up a fight with the intruder, both Barry and Ashley believed the murderer was voluntarily admitted to the home without fear of danger. Ashley believed someone had called the victims beforehand.

Herb's phone records were clean. He had not called any of the murder victims.

She and Barry had fleeting thoughts that Moseley himself could be involved. Would publicity about murder victims help or hurt radio listenership?

Moseley's background checks went as smoothly as any she had ever done. Bank accounts, phone records, living expenses—Mike Moseley was Mr. Clean. Every single aspect of his background was transparent, sensible and honest. Ashley would bet her last dollar on Moseley's integrity.

Then she looked at the other left-leaners at WBEO. Most lived payday to payday; several had maxed-out credit cards and no savings; they voted for and supported far-left politicians, but it was a stretch to conclude that any of them would resort to violence.

Thomas Brody, the irate investor who seemed to be a self-appointed spokesman for Nutley's investors, is a successful businessman, well respected, works long hours, with never a hint of wrong doing. Furthermore, his bone to pick was with Nutley, not Moseley.

Ashley turned her attention next to the D. C. law firm that clearly wants Moseley off the air. She checked for employees and independent contractors who do work for the firm. She came up with hundreds of names, a dozen or so in every major city in the country. It would require weeks to complete a background check on this gang, and she and Barry had promised results in just two weeks, and most of that period had already passed. Her conclusion was the first option was still at work—paying off Moseley to give up his program. If that doesn't work, they may activate the goon squad. Should that occur, expect anything, including murder. But she doubted that phase of the operation had begun.

Howard Nutley's records were far from being pure and upright. He had called the victims' numbers in Pittsburgh, Kansas City, Denver and St. Louis, but not the number in Indianapolis.

Ashley now feels more certain a charge against Nutley could be upheld in the four murder cases. But not the Indianapolis case. Someone else is involved.

Nutley's bank account records were nearly impossible to interpret. Customers' funds and his personal funds had been comingled, a clear violation of law. State laws require that customer funds be deposited in a separate trust or escrow account. Millions of dollars had been deposited into his personal account. Much of this may have come from new investors. Some of it may have come from someone paying him to murder conservative listeners. It will be an accounting nightmare to unscramble such a mess. SEC auditors will have their hands full. Perhaps they will be able to figure it out over the next few weeks.

Everything was checking out just about as Ashley had imagined. Suddenly Ashley saw it clearly. She was absolutely certain she can now identify the person who had been directing Nutley's activities and who is ultimately responsible for the murders. She made a checklist of the things she had yet to do to tie it down once and for all.

Barry's plane was due in from New Orleans at 4 p.m. today. She was certain Barry would be pleased with the progress she has made. If he agrees with her analysis, their investigation will soon come to a close.

26.

"Are you sitting down?" Mike Moseley was on the phone. "I'm afraid I've got more bad news. There's been another murder, this one in Louisville."

"Yes, I know," Ashley answered.

"You know? How do you know?"

"We have our ways. I'll explain to you later. When can we meet with you and Zack Forrester? We've got important news for you."

"As you know, I never have a minute to spare until I go off the air. How about right after today's program?"

"Yes, I think our news can wait. We'll see you at 4 o'clock today."

———◼︎———

Just before four Barry, Ashley, Columbus Detective Payton Snyder, and FBI Agent Dennis Connor showed up at the WBEO studios and were escorted to the station's conference room.

A caller was elucidating on global warming. "Everybody knows it's a problem, everybody keeps talking about it, but nobody does anything about it. It's time we solve this problem once and for all."

"Nobody wants the earth to become too warm," Moseley answered, "but are you sure we're experiencing man-made global warming?"

"Of course, I'm sure. We're having more storms, more wild fires, more droughts, and other disasters. It's serious."

"I'm afraid this is another example of inaccurate news

getting disseminated," Moseley commented. "Historical analyses show the number of wildfires has decreased by 15% since 1950; the world has not experienced an increase in the number of droughts; and we're seeing the lowest level of severe landfall hurricanes in more than a hundred years.

"Global warming gets a lot of bad press. It has been blamed for malaria, the Minneapolis bridge collapse, teenage drinking, terrorism, too much snow, too little snow, the Atlantic ocean becoming less salty, the Atlantic becoming more salty, the earth slowing down, the earth speeding up, bigger fish, smaller fish, better beer, worse beer, and even the irritability of mice. I wondered what was wrong with those little devils.

"Today the polar bear population is increasing, not declining as widely reported, and while some glaciers are melting, others are growing.

"There have been warming trends, and cooling trends, for 3,000 years. There have been five extended periods when the atmosphere was warmer than it is today. Today's temperatures remain below the 3,000 year average."

"The next thing you'll be telling me is that we're experiencing global cooling," the caller said.

"That could be. In the early 1970s scientists were concerned about global cooling. They predicted the next ice age. The world's population was going to starve because we would not be able to grow crops on the ice cap. Global cooling was the lead story featured on the cover of *Time* magazine on June 24, 1974. Check it out the next time you're at your dentist's office. Keep in mind that at one time Greenland was green. Now it's 85% covered by ice."

"How come I'm just now hearing about this?"

"The news media lives on news releases, not their own

research. And global warming stuff is what several interest groups are spewing out in their news releases. The next time you read about global warming, look at the source. It's generally one of these: (1) Researchers who are getting taxpayer money to do studies on global warming, or climate change as they call it now. Global warming can be disputed, but no one can question climate change. Climates change every day. Obviously these folks want tax money to keep rolling in so they can continue to do research until the day they die. (2) Companies that make wind mills, solar panels, and the like. They see this as a new, expanding market, and who can blame them? They want climate change to be real. (3) Politicians who are drooling to find a new tax they can impose on the American people—a tax that's sort of hidden. What could be better than a carbon tax that corporations have to build into the prices they charge? With a new built-in tax, corporations get blamed for higher prices and the politicians don't get blamed for increasing income taxes on people who are already hurting."

"You're saying I can't trust the newspapers and TV news?" the caller asked.

"I'm saying you must be very selective and do some research on your own. Read news accounts from several sources. A lot of inaccurate news is being circulated."

Several times during Moseley's comments the FBI agent and the Columbus detective interjected their own commentary—"Thataway!" "It's about time somebody in the media told the truth." It was clear they truly enjoyed the interchange.

When Moseley's program ended, he and station manager Forrester came into the conference room. Barry made appropriate introductions.

"You're here about the Louisville murder?" Forrester

asked.

"We have checked out the Louisville murder with the police department there," Barry answered, "and we have found the Louisville murder followed the Indianapolis pattern precisely. The victim lived alone; no evidence of forcible entry or victim resistance; the *2morrow* inscription inked on the victim's forehead; fingerprints had been wiped clean and usable DNA destroyed. The victim was a political conservative, and a check of program tapes confirmed that he had called Moseley's program.

"The murder formula had worked well in the past, and the murderer in this case stuck with it to the nth degree.

"There were two notable differences from the first four murders. Comparing pictures of the inscriptions on the victims' foreheads, the graphologist we employed is totally certain the inscription was made by the same person who had made the inscription in Indianapolis.

"Also," Barry continued, "the same hand gun was used in the Indianapolis and Louisville murders—a .38 caliber Smith and Wesson Model 10. The ballistics print is exactly the same, unlike the first four murders in which a different weapon had been used in each."

"How do you know the make and model of the hand gun?" Moseley asked.

"We'll get to that in a minute," Barry answered.

"This tells us the murderer did not fly aboard commercial aircraft to Indianapolis and Louisville. The murderer drove."

"Who might that be?" Moseley asked.

"Mr. Forrester, you were not in your office on the dates of the two murders," Barry said.

"I have a seven-day-a-week job. I don't get weekends off like most people. I take a day now and then, often in the middle of the week."

"But you were in Louisville the day of that murder?" Ashley asked.

"What makes you think I was in Louisville?"

"I placed a GPS device on your car. We know precisely where you drove, where you made stops, and for how long."

"Is that legal?" Forrester asked.

No one answered.

"You were in Louisville on that date?" Ashley asked again.

"I have friends in Louisville. I visit them once in a while."

"Name the friends you were visiting on that date," Ashley continued.

"It was...ah...ah.... Where I drive doesn't mean a thing. This is a free country. I can drive where and when I please. If I stopped anyplace close to the murder scene, it was purely a coincidence.

"You're trying to pin these murders on me? I have no reason to want to murder anybody," Forrester barked.

"First of all," Ashley said, "you have a far-left political ideology. Because of your role as manager of this station and as the station's public face in this community, executives at the Communicator Radio Corporation in Houston, the owner of this station, asked you to cool it. At their request you agreed to take a neutral stance."

"So what?" Forrester answered argumentatively. "Everybody has certain beliefs. This doesn't mean anyone would resort to murder."

"From the outset, you have wanted the *Tomorrow* program off the air. Because of its popularity and its success as the biggest revenue producer for this station, Communicator Radio Corporation has vetoed your suggestion."

"That doesn't mean a thing. Selecting programs we air on

this station is a matter of judgment. Nothing is a sure thing. So we have disagreed from time to time. So what?"

"And you have disagreed strongly with station management on salaries. You have argued that you should be earning more as station manager than Mr. Moseley earns as a talk show host. The owners have ignored your arguments, and you have not taken this lightly."

"Salaries are often discussed. Everybody thinks they ought to be earning more. What's this got to do with murders?"

"You and Howard Nutley, both having a left-wing ideology, concocted a plan to draw listeners away from the program by having loyal listeners murdered. For the first four murders, Nutley pulled the trigger and you paid him. Your bank records show a transfer of $25,000 prior to each murder."

"Oh come on, for Christ's sake! This was money given to Nutley for investment. He had an excellent track record of making good investments for his clients, and I wanted to be a part of it."

"You provided the phone numbers of conservative callers to Mr. Nutley. Your phone in your office is the only phone in the studios having a caller ID feature for all incoming lines except for the phone of your call screener."

"The fancy phone goes with the job. It doesn't mean a thing."

Barry picked up on the conversation. "Here is a copy of a letter you will find interesting. Howard Nutley left it in a New Orleans hotel room where he was registered as Harold Guest. He has taken his own life with a .38 caliber hand gun. In the room were driver's licenses and credit cards bearing three names—Howard Nutley, Carl Bristol, and Harold Guest. Graphologists have reviewed this letter and have confirmed it is written in Nutley's own hand.

To my friends and associates,

I have much to apologize for. Although many of my wrongs cannot be corrected, hopefully over time some of my injustices can be forgiven.

I must start with my investors, most of whom I have known for years, some since high school and college. I held myself out as an astute investor who could produce profits not possible elsewhere in the investment world. I apologize for having deceived you. With your money I made some average investments not unlike those anyone could have made with little or no investment experience. The remainder I used to finance a lifestyle that enhanced my ego—a lifestyle I could not otherwise afford. Hopefully some of your investments can be recovered. I'm afraid that much of your money will be lost forever. Again, I apologize.

More recently 30 new investors have agreed to give me $300 million to invest for them. Hopefully it isn't too late to suspend these investments. I'm sorry to have misled you.

Since early in life I have had a left-leaning political philosophy. Mike Moseley's conservative talk show has always annoyed me. As a result, Zack Forrester, a long-time friend, and I came up with a plan intended to damage his listenership. If conservative callers were murdered, and the murders were highly publicized across the country, we believed the American people would stop listening to Moseley's program. They would be fearful of being added to the murder list. Zack agreed to pay me $25,000 for each conservative listener whose life was taken in accordance with the plan we devised.

These were good people, kind people, people with fine families, people who didn't deserve what they got. I apologize to their families.

Greed knows no bounds. I could not get enough money, so I tried to blackmail Zack Forrester. Zack has been a good friend, a long-time friend, a friend who has supported my efforts to promote liberal causes. Zack, I'm glad you did not respond to my demands. I apologize to you, my friend.

Stephen Bower, my associate, was the first to learn of our plan to murder conservative listeners. Our cubicle walls at our offices are thin. There are not many secrets, and Stephen overheard a phone conversation. He approached me in a very gentlemanly manner, so typical of Stephen. He didn't want me to hurt others or to damage my own career. He meant well. I thought if I took Stephen's life, no one would learn of our plan and all my problems would be behind me. I should have known better. My apologies to his wife and family.

I'm sure there are others I've forgotten. I've hurt so many people. There is no way I can correct my wrongs. I feel there is only one course of action. I must make the ultimate sacrifice with my own life.

If it's within your hearts, please forgive me.

Howard M. Nutley

Forrester read the letter. Then he read it again.

"This doesn't mean a thing," he said. "Nutley has proved himself to be a liar. He lied to his clients; he lied to everybody; and he's lying in this letter. He has proven he can't be trusted. His word is no good."

"Since Nutley left his business and went on the run, there was nobody to pursue the plan to damage Mike's radio listenership, so you picked up the mantle," Barry said. "You murdered the listeners in Indianapolis and Louisville."

"That's insane. How do you come up with all this nonsense? What a fairy tale!"

"Two days ago a court order was obtained to search your home for two firearms. Both were found—a .38 caliber Smith and Wesson Model 10 whose bullets produced identical ballistics markings as the bullets in the Louisville and Indianapolis murders.

"We also checked out your Remington 700 high powered rifle whose .30-06 bullets were found in Howard Nutley's house siding. You took shots at Nutley after he tried to blackmail you. And you used this rifle to take shots at Ashley and me, apparently to encourage us to withdraw from the case.

"In addition, you forced Nutley's car off the road and then abandoned the rental car in a downtown garage. Your DNA was found in the rental. Also, the rental agent has identified your picture as the person who rented the car."

Forrester was shocked. He was pale. He looked toward the floor. He didn't speak.

FBI Agent Connor took a small card from his pocket and began to read:

You have the right to remain silent. Anything you say can and will be used against you in a court of law. You have the right to talk to a lawyer and have him present with you while you are being questioned. If you cannot afford to hire a lawyer, one will be appointed to represent you before any questioning if you wish. You can decide at any time to exercise these rights and not answer any questions or make any statement. Do you understand each of these rights I have explained to you?

Forrester sat, with head down, and did not respond. He knew his career and his comfortable life had ended.

27.

"Ashley, we've got a check for you," Mike Moseley said on the phone. "I suppose you and Barry will insist on being paid and are not going to work just for the experience."

"We haven't discussed it lately, but chances are the vote will be 2-0 toward getting paid. We have become accustomed to a steady diet of food and regular shelter, although we know that's extravagant. We have become terribly spoiled."

"Can you come over at the regular time?"

"Yes we can. We'll be there."

Barry and Ashley listened to Moseley's program on the car radio on the way to the studios. Interestingly, no caller asked about the arrest of Zack Forrester, the master mind behind the plot to get Moseley off the air.

"I'm concerned about entitlements," Josh of Houston said. "It's hard to be openly critical of what American taxpayers are spending to help the most unfortunate because people think we're selfish or hard hearted. Yet costs are getting out of hand."

"Your point is well taken," Moseley answered. "It's a problem that has to be solved. The legitimate needy must be taken care of with a workable safety net, but there has to be a way of eliminating the abuse."

"The Bureau of Economic Analysis doesn't even know how many government agencies dispense benefits to the American people. Nobody can figure it out. That alone should tell you we have a problem. They do know we spend $2.3 trillion a year to help the so-called needy. Of course, that must be paid for with taxes or by borrowing more money. And the borrowing has to be paid for eventually by taxpayers."

"The fact that we don't even know how many federal agencies are involved helps explain the cost problem," Josh added. "If we ask politicians to make the process more efficient, they'll probably recommend the formation of another federal agency."

"That $2.3 trillion," Moseley continued, "amounts to $7,400 for every American man, woman and child. But we must remember that half of American families pay no taxes. Therefore, the average American family of four that pays taxes is responsible for $29,600 a year to help the people who either legitimately need help or who won't work."

"That's the distinction that bothers me most," Josh added. "I'm willing to help take care of people who need help. But I resent taking care of people who are the dregs of society, people who are better able to work than I am and who take advantage of programs intended for the truly needy."

"Good point, Josh. The American people are very generous, the most generous of any people in the world. They are willing to help those who need help. But they resent the cheaters and they resent political corruption.

"The Bureau of Labor Statistics says the number of adult men age 20 and older working or seeking work has dropped 13% between 1948 and 2008. Today 7% of men in their late 30s, which is the primary working age in America, have totally checked out of the workforce. A major reason is the flight to government disability programs. In December 2012 there were 8.8 million people drawing Social Security disability benefits, nearly three times as many as in December 1990. For every 17 people who are working, there is one drawing Social Security disability.

"And there are disability programs beyond Social Security.

In total some 12.4 million working-age people draw some form of disability from government programs. There are only some 150 million working people in the United States. In other words, more than 8% of American working people claim to be disabled."

"How can we go about fixing the problem?" Josh asked.

"In my view, we must do two things. First, consolidate the federal programs so there is one source for disability benefits. With so many overlapping programs, no one agency knows what benefits are being paid by other agencies. It's difficult to recognize abuse. Second, tighten eligibility to squeeze out the cheaters."

Moseley's program came to an end just as Barry and Ashley pulled into the station's parking lot.

Joining Moseley, Barry and Ashley in the conference room was Herb Bentley.

"Here's your check," Moseley said. "I'm very pleased with your work, and the top dog at Communicator Communications is pleased as well. Congratulations on a job well done."

"We think all the pieces of the puzzle have been laid to rest, with the possible exception of our D.C. lawyer friend, Mr. Fogleman," Barry said.

"I should have mentioned that Mr. Fogleman has been in touch again. He is still insisting I give up my program. I told him I would not give up my program under any circumstance and that if he continued to put pressure on me, I'd make him famous.

"He was surprised that I knew how many goons he had working for him in various cities around the country. I used your research and didn't give you credit for it. Sorry 'bout that."

"The information is yours," Ashley answered. "You paid for it."

"I outlined some of the dirty tricks that we might expect, and I told him that we will make this a countrywide issue that will disgust every American voter and turn them against his tactics. I don't expect him to give up that easily, but maybe he'll think twice before he gives us too hard a time."

"I want to thank you too," Herb Bentley said. "You know, I've been a liberal all my life. My grandparents were liberals, my parents were liberals, and that's the only political philosophy I'd ever heard.

"When I went to work for Mike, for the first time I heard two sides of the story, but my job was mechanical. I tried to put different viewpoints on the air, but my job was balance. I don't know that I understood the facts. I just wanted to air pros and cons on every issue. I didn't try to interpret the facts. I continued to make my judgments on the basis of family background and emotion, not facts.

"But the problems Mike has faced, and an understanding of the measures some people are willing to take to shut down one viewpoint, made me realize there are certain people in this country who want a government-controlled media, just like countries run by dictators. I've been thinking a lot about it, how our system of government can't continue as it is now. I've begun to consider the mess I'm leaving for my kids. I have finally realized I'm not a liberal. I'm a conservative—a person who believes in freedom, opportunities for advancement, and for the right to pull oneself up. Mike, I'm one of your advocates. I hope I haven't embarrassed you in any way."

"No, you haven't embarrassed me," Mike answered. "You've done a good job for us. I'm just pleased you're a convert. Now if we can get just 26,999,999 others to join you."

The Author

Bob Bailey is the retired CEO of a major company. Under his leadership the company he headed became one of the top performing property and casualty insurance companies in the United States.

By his own account, he failed retirement and, at his wife's urging, wrote his first book, *Plain Talk About Leadership*. That was followed by two other business books, *The New Leader* and *Super-Size Your Sales*.

He then turned his attention to self-help books, *What Do You Do When You're Having a Bad Day* and *The Poverty Advantage*.

"You read too many business books," his wife told him, "and you read very few novels. Why don't you write a novel?" So he did. *Baja Outlaw* was published in 2012. And now this one, *The 1-800 Murders*.

For additional information about the author, visit
www.bobbaileyspeaker.com
or contact him at bobbailey1@comcast.net
or 941-358-5260.
He is always interested in your feedback.